THE TRILOGY OF FRIGHT™

ERIK SHEIN **MELISSA DAVIS** **KAREN FULLER**

World Castle Publishing, LLC
Pensacola, Florida
Copyright © 2024 Shein Partnership, LLC
Authors: Erik Shein, Melissa Davis & Karen Fuller
Hardback ISBN: 9798345036747
Paperback ISBN: 9798891263055
First Edition World Castle Publishing, LLC, October 31, 2024
http://www.worldcastlepublishing.com

Cover Art: Cover Designs by Karen
Cover-designs-by-karen.com

FRIGHTWRITTEN

ERIK
SHEIN
MELISSA
DAVIS
KAREN
FULLER

CHAPTER 1
FRIGHTWRITTEN

The steam hissed like a ghostly whisper as I carefully crafted another heart in the frothy surface of a customer's cappuccino. The irony wasn't lost on me — here I was, creating art in milk while my own artistic abilities lay dormant and unused.

The rhythmic hum of the coffee shop surrounded me, a constant reminder of the monotony that had consumed my life. Each jingle of the doorbell only served to underscore how the world kept moving forward while I remained trapped in place.

My break beckoned like a haunting melody, and I retreated to the sanctuary of the back room, a blank notebook clutched tightly in my hands. Its empty pages taunted me, reflecting my own perceived lack of potential. Despite my best efforts, I could only scrawl meaningless words onto the pristine sheets — a fruitless dance leading nowhere.

"Come on, you've got this," I whispered, trying to psych myself up. "Your creativity's still in there somewhere." But even as I said it, doubt crept in, clinging to me like a stubborn shadow. No matter how I tried to reason with myself, that nagging feeling just wouldn't let go.

It was in this hollow daze that my phone shattered the silence with its harsh ringtone. With a resigned sigh, I answered, already knowing who was on the other end.

"Hi, Mom," I answered, steeling myself for the conversation ahead.

"Claire, we read your...article," she said, her tone

heavy with disappointment. "When are you going to give up this writing thing and get a real job?"

"Writing is a real job," I replied, my voice wavering despite my attempt to sound confident.

"Your father and I just want you to be happy — stable," she pressed on, her words sharp under a veneer of concern. "A proper career, a family...not these creative pursuits."

"I'm not twelve anymore. Writing not some childish phase," I argued, gripping the phone tighter. "And I don't need a family to prove I'm doing okay."

There was a pause, a moment of frosty silence. "We'll see," she finally said, then hung up. I set the phone down with shaky hands, the quiet now even more oppressive than before.

In the wake of that call, something inside me hardened. Their doubts, their expectations — I wouldn't let them define me. I'd forge my own path, rocky and uncertain as it might be, but at least it would be mine.

As I headed back to the front, to the familiar hiss of the espresso machine and the hum of customers' chatter, the chime of the bell went off as the mailman entered the cafe. I felt a new determination burning in my chest. I'd write my story, and it would be a farewell to the ordinary life they wanted for me — a life I was now more set than ever on leaving behind.

The café's bell chimed again as the postman left, leaving behind an ornate envelope that looked out of place in our modest coffee shop. I ran my fingers over the fancy seal, feeling the weight of history in the thick paper. Aunt Eleanor — the name drifted through my mind like a half-forgotten memory.

"What's that?" Jake asked, glancing up from the espresso machine with mild interest.

"It's from my aunt's attorney. She passed away about

six months ago," I said, carefully opening the envelope. "She was a writer. Lived alone in some secluded cottage upstate."

"Sounds like quite the character," Jake remarked, but his light tone couldn't lift the sadness settling over me.

"Yeah." I unfolded the letter, my eyes darting over the words. 'Inheritance'... 'Cottage'... 'Literary estate.' The realization hit me like a bolt of lightning. "I don't believe this."

"What? She leave you something?"

"Yeah...her house."

"Whoa, Claire, that's...that's huge!"

"Or a huge mistake," I muttered. But inside, something shifted, like the pieces of a puzzle finally clicking into place.

Later, in my cramped apartment — surrounded by stacks of books and the lingering scent of put-off dreams — I stood amid the remnants of a life I'd settled for. My hand shook as I dialed the number, each press of a button feeling weightier than the last.

"Hey, Marty, it's Claire," I said into the phone, my voice barely above a whisper. "I'm calling to... I'm quitting. Effective immediately."

Marty sputtered into the phone. "Wait, what? Now? But—"

"I know, I was supposed to open tomorrow. Jake can handle it." I sat down on the edge of the couch. "Look, I know it's sudden, but I'm moving upstate."

"Moving?" I could hear the frustration in his voice. "Why am I just hearing about this now?"

"I just found out today — I inherited a house," I replied calmly. "This move...it's the right thing for me."

"Are you sure about this, Claire?" My manager sounded both worried and annoyed. "Is there anything we can do to change your mind?"

"No," I cut in, surprising myself with my firmness. The

imaginary hold of my parents' expectations seemed to loosen its grip. "This is something I've got to do."

The phone clicked as I set it down, the sound marking the end of one chapter and the beginning of another. I turned to my belongings, packing them up with a strange sense of detachment. Each item felt like a piece of a life that had never quite fit.

As night fell, I found myself diving into the online world of Eleanor Hargrave. Her face stared back at me from the screen, pale and serious, her eyes seeming to hold untold stories. An eerie stillness settled over me as I read about her writing career, her interest in the occult, and her secluded final years.

"Well, Aunt Eleanor," I murmured to the quiet room, almost feeling her presence in the flickering light of my desk lamp. "Let's see what you've left for me." Before sunrise, I had packed up the last of my things, my heart racing with a mix of excitement and fear for the uncertain path ahead, towards a place where reality and fantasy might start to blur.

In the quiet pre-dawn hours, I took one last look at the life I was leaving behind. My heart pounded with a mix of dread and anticipation, Eleanor's mysterious legacy pulling me forward. It was time to step into the unknown, to face whatever ghosts — real or imagined — awaited me, and to write the story that had been lurking in the shadows all along.

With the last box sealed, I took a deep breath, my eyes lingering on the empty apartment. The decision had been made; there was no turning back now. I grabbed my keys, turned off the lights one last time, and stepped out into the chilly morning air. The drive ahead was long, but every mile would take me closer to the answers I sought.

The veil of mist parted reluctantly as my tires crunched the gravel beneath them, the rhythmic percussion a stark contrast to the silence that hung heavy over the countryside. I'd driven for hours, yet the journey felt like a mere continuation of the countless roads I had traversed in my mind — each one leading to this inevitable destination. Aunt Eleanor's cottage, with its gothic silhouette, emerged from the shroud of fog as if conjured by some arcane ritual.

I killed the engine, and the sudden quietude wrapped around me like a shawl. As I stepped out, the earthy scent of damp soil and decayed leaves infiltrated my senses, the air thick with whispers from the past. The cottage stood as a sentinel, windows like vacant eyes overseeing the gnarled trees that encroached upon it, their branches clawing at the sides in a silent plea for entry.

My heart beat a staccato rhythm against my ribs, each pulse echoing Eleanor's cryptic legacy. With every step toward the front door, the weight of her absence bore down on me, the gravity of my own solitude pressing into my skin. My fingers fumbled for the key — a cold, metallic promise — and as I grasped it, the texture bit into my palm, grounding me in the reality of my decision.

"This better be worth it," I murmured to myself, the words barely escaping before being swallowed by the oppressive atmosphere. Excitement and apprehension warred within me, my ambitious dreams clashing with the specter of self-doubt that always lingered at the fringes of my mind.

With a deep breath that did little to steady my nerves, I turned the key, the lock protesting with a groan that seemed to emanate from the very bowels of the house. Pushing open the door, a gust of stale air greeted me, carrying the musty perfume of forgotten tales and secret sorrows. I stepped over the threshold, the darkness beyond beckoning me into its embrace.

This was my new life — a sanctuary bequeathed to

me by a woman whose enigmatic aura had seeped into the stone and timber. I closed the door behind me, sealing myself within the walls that harbored Eleanor's essence. The silence was no longer just an absence of sound; it was an entity, alive and pulsing, wrapping its invisible tendrils around my consciousness.

I stood there, in the liminal space between the world I knew and the one that awaited, ready to unravel the mysteries that hummed beneath the surface. Little did I know, the story I sought to write would soon become indistinguishable from the haunting narrative that the cottage, with its spectral whispers and shadows, was eager to tell.

CHAPTER 2
FRIGHTWRITTEN

I awoke to the stern caress of morning light, dissecting the room through narrow cracks in the curtains. Long shadows stretched like fingers across the floor, beckoning me into an unfamiliar dance with daybreak. I sat up, my heart pulsing erratically against the cloak of silence suffocating the cottage. It was as though the very air held its breath, waiting for my next move.

Draping my feet over the side of the bed, I rose, each step an intrusion upon the hallowed stillness. The wooden floor groaned beneath my weight, whispering secrets of forgotten footsteps. My hand trailed along the spines of dusty books that lined the shelves, each a silent sentinel guarding Eleanor's reclusive existence.

Through dim corridors, I moved, drawn forward by an insatiable curiosity that gnawed at the edges of my reason. The air grew thick with the musk of old paper and the ghost of lavender perfume — a scent I imagined Eleanor herself might have worn. Every antique clock I passed stood motionless, their pendulums stilled, marking not the passage of time but its eerie cessation. It was odd. Every clock was stopped at the same time — 3 o'clock.

Each room unfurled another layer of my aunt's solitude, her life etched into the very fabric of the house. A knitting basket lay abandoned by a rocking chair, needles poised mid-stitch as if she'd simply vanished mid-thought. Portraits hung on the walls, her sharp blue eyes following my every move, challenging me to delve deeper into her enigmatic world.

Then, there it was — the heavy oak door, more a barrier to a sacred realm than a mere entryway. My palms pressed against the wood, feeling the grain's ancient stories pulse beneath my touch. It gave way with a protest, hinges singing a discordant hymn, revealing the sanctum of Eleanor Hargrave.

The study lay before me, untouched since her departure from this mortal coil. Gossamer webs adorned corners like tattered lace, and dust motes pirouetted in the shafts of light that dared penetrate the gloom. I let out a heavy sigh. This would be a major chore to clean. "What a mess." The room was chaos incarnate — piles of papers, half-burned candles, and books strewn about as if discarded in some fervent search for forbidden knowledge.

There, amid the clutter, stood the crown jewel of her possessions: a massive, ornate desk. Its surface was a tableau of neglect, dust veiling its secrets like the first frost of winter. I tugged at a drawer. "Locked. Of course." The desk stood as a silent guardian of Eleanor's final words, a siren call to my writer's soul. I scanned the room, muttering, "Where'd she stash the damn key?" Its absence, the desk's contents hidden away in this enigmatic space, only stoked the fire of my curiosity. "What were you hiding, Aunt Eleanor?"

The longer I gazed upon the desk, the more I felt an inexplicable kinship with its departed mistress. We were both prisoners of our own minds — she to her creations, and I to my self-doubt. Yet here, in the heart of her sanctuary, I found a perverse comfort, as if the tendrils of her spirit lingered, intertwining with my own.

Was it my ambition that led me forward, or some darker compulsion? Whichever the case may be, I could not resist the allure. For what is a writer but a conduit for the voices of the past, desperate to be heard through the annals of time?

I turned from the desk, its secrets jealously guarded by that stubborn lock, and began rifling through Eleanor's belongings with a fervor that bordered on the indecent. My fingers, nimble and intrusive, overturned every book and every parchment as if the very act of searching could dispel the mist of unease that clung to the air like cobwebs.

"Where are you hiding?" I muttered to myself — or to Eleanor's ghost, should it be listening with an ethereal ear. The room seemed to tighten around me, the walls inching closer with each ticking second, as though they, too, were eager for the revelation.

Then, amidst a pile of leather-bound volumes on the occult, my hand brushed against a tome whose spine gave way too easily. A hollowed-out sanctuary within the pages cradled a key, small and unassuming, yet it thrummed with potential as I held it aloft. The metal was cold, a silent echo of the tomb-like study. With hesitant reverence, I approached the desk once more.

A breath I hadn't realized I'd been holding escaped as the key slid into the lock with an ease that felt preordained. The drawer creaked open, a sound that resonated deeper than it should have, stirring the dust motes into a frenzied dance.

There it lay: Eleanor's unfinished manuscript, the edges of the pages yellowed with age, yet the ink as stark as if it had been penned yesterday. The sight of it sent a jolt through me, a connection tethering me to the woman who had crafted these words.

I sank into her chair, the leather groaning under my weight, a protest or perhaps a welcome — it was hard to tell. The first page beckoned, and I succumbed, my eyes devouring the opening lines.

"Darkness is not simply the absence of light," I read aloud, my voice a stranger in this tomb of creativity. "It is a living thing, a cloak that both conceals and reveals the truths we dare not face."

With each sentence, the room grew colder, the shadows stretching towards me as if drawn by the tale unfolding beneath my fingertips. And then, with a sharp intake of breath, the realization struck — a description of a young woman standing at the edge of an abyss, her heart a maelstrom of ambition and doubt. It was me.

The manuscript was a mirror, reflecting parts of my soul I had kept hidden even from myself. Eleanor had laid bare a narrative so intimately familiar that it clawed at the inside of my skull, demanding attention, whispering of kinship.

"Who were you, Eleanor?" I whispered, my voice trembling with newfound kinship and fear. "And what have you left behind for me to find?"

As I turned the page, the wind outside picked up a mournful howl, as if the cottage itself was reading over my shoulder, eager for the story to continue. The line between Eleanor's world and mine blurred, and I was no longer certain where one ended and the other began.

I traced my fingers over the words, each sentence a revelation, each paragraph a confession. Time slipped away, lost in the labyrinth of Eleanor's narrative. As I delved deeper into the manuscript, the lines on the page blurred into a symphony of shared experiences and mirrored emotions.

The last vestiges of daylight had succumbed to the encroaching night, and only the small desk lamp kept the shadows at bay. The study was a mausoleum of thoughts, and I, a solitary mourner amidst its cryptic whispers. Eleanor's words had seeped into my marrow, stirring embers of creativity long thought extinguished. With trembling hands,

I caressed the manuscript — its pages were the gateway to an unfinished legacy.

I peered through the window, seeking counsel from the stars, but found only a velvet darkness that mirrored the abyss within my own soul. A sigh escaped me, frosted breath coalescing with the chill of the room — a chill that seemed to emanate from the very walls themselves. There it was again, that peculiar sensation; the cottage breathed with an anticipatory silence as if waiting for my next move.

My heart, once shackled by doubt, now beat with a fervor that demanded release. "Eleanor," I murmured to the emptiness, "your tale will not languish in obscurity." The decision alighted upon me like a specter, at once exhilarating and ominous. Yes, I would finish what she began. Her work, her passion, her legacy — it was now intertwined with mine, our fates indelibly inked upon the same parchment.

As I settled back into the chair, a relic that bore the imprint of Eleanor's resolve, I poised my pen over the blank expanse of paper. A silent prayer, or perhaps a curse, slipped from my lips, and then the dam broke. Words cascaded forth, spilling onto the page with a fervor that bordered on possession. Sentences wove themselves into paragraphs, paragraphs into pages, each one a step deeper into the heart of the narrative — a narrative that was becoming eerily more personal with every stroke of the pen.

Time slipped away, meaningless in the grip of creative frenzy. The fading daylight painted eerie patterns across the walls, transforming familiar shapes into ghostly silhouettes. I could almost hear Eleanor's voice in the soft groan of the old floorboards, her presence — encouragement or caution? — whispering in the rustle of leaves against the windowpane.

Something shifted. The air grew denser, laden with a presence that was at once foreign and intimately known.

My chest tightened, a premonition crawling up my spine, whispering that this path I embarked upon was fraught with peril. But the story beckoned, a siren call that would not be ignored. I leaned into its embrace, heedless of the looming shadows that gathered around me, hungry for the tale that would be born from the union of two haunted souls.

"Forgive me, Eleanor," I found myself saying, the words an incantation in the gloom. "But your ghosts are now mine to bear."

And so, beneath the watchful gaze of the moon, hidden behind its shroud of clouds, I wrote. I wrote until the boundary between Claire Monroe and Eleanor Hargrave blurred into nothingness until the whispers of the past became indistinguishable from the cries of the present. The manuscript was a conduit, and through it flowed the terrors and triumphs of a life suspended between two realms — one living, one spectral.

"Let the horrors come," I challenged the silence. "I am ready."

The last rays of sunlight faded, plunging the room into darkness, and at that moment, I knew my fate was sealed. The cottage, Eleanor, the manuscript — they had claimed me, binding me to a story that would consume me entirely. Yet, I embraced this all-encompassing passion with open arms.

CHAPTER 3
FRIGHTWRITTEN

The pen flowed effortlessly as I wove words into the fabric of Eleanor's unfinished saga. My thoughts spilled onto the pages, a delicate thread stitching my narrative to hers — two stories mysteriously intertwined. Scattered papers covered the desk, our handwriting mingling across the sheets. I was crafting a tale of a young woman, not unlike myself, lost within the winding corridors of an ancestral home she had never known. The parallels whispered to me, soft and insidious, as if Eleanor's ghost hovered at my shoulder, guiding my hand.

The cottage groaned around me, its bones settling into the twilight hour, or so I told myself. But as dusk deepened into night, a peculiar unease coiled within me. My gaze lifted from the manuscript, and I stretched stiff limbs, the silence of the room punctuated only by the ticking of the old grandfather clock. I wandered through the dim corridors, the whispers of the house — and perhaps something more — echoing in my ears.

Light flickered a capricious dance that made the walls pulse as if the cottage itself drew breath. My heart stuttered, mirroring the erratic sputter of the bulbs above. "Must be faulty wiring," I muttered, a feeble attempt to quell the rising dread. Yet, at that moment, a whisper caressed my ear, ethereal as cobweb on skin. A voice? No, surely just the wind's playful sigh against the windowpane.

Compelled by a curiosity that often proved my master, I traced the sound to its source. The empty living room offered no answers, only the quiet mockery of my own reflection in the dusty mirror. I laughed, hollow and brief, at the trickery of my senses. How easily the mind conjured phantoms when steeped in tales of terror. Eleanor, you've bewitched me with your macabre tales, I thought, shaking my head at my own fanciful notions.

Yet even as I dismissed the occurrences, a seed of doubt took root in the furrows of my mind, sprouting tendrils of unease that I could not fully shake. The whispers of the cottage, the echoes of my own story, they melded into a chorus that set the rhythm of my pulse racing. With each step back to the sanctuary of my writing desk, I felt the weight of unseen eyes, the breath of silent watchers upon my neck.

I resumed my work with fervor, attempting to drown the disquiet in the flow of ink. But the sense of déjà vu clung to me, a shroud I could not cast off. And in the stillness of the night, between the lines of Eleanor's legacy and my own burgeoning tale, the boundary began to blur.

The whispers grew louder, more insistent, slithering through the dark emptiness of each room. I glanced around, eyes darting to each shadowy corner, expecting to find the source of the spectral murmurs. Yet only stillness and dust greeted my gaze.

My heart thudded, breath came quicker. "It's just my imagination," I muttered through clenched teeth. But the insidious voices continued, now accompanied by faint scuttling sounds, like long-fingered hands scrabbling over the floorboards.

I whirled around. "Who's there?" My cry echoed through the cottage, the only response. Fingers trembling, I reached for the manuscript, seeking comfort in Eleanor's words. But the pages were blank, every line erased. I froze, skin prickling with unease.

The temperature dropped abruptly, a bone-deep chill settling into the walls. My own breath misted before me as shadowy forms gathered at the edges of my vision. This was no mere figment of an overwrought mind. Some malevolent presence haunted this place, seeping from the very bones of the cottage.

I backed away, pulse thundering in my ears. This was madness. And yet a part of me thrilled at the mystery unfolding, the tale I had become ensnared in. My fate now intertwined with Eleanor's, our stories merging into one harrowing descent into the darkness.

A loud bang woke me where I'd fallen asleep at the desk. I sat up with a start, blinking in the dim light. For a moment, I was disoriented, unsure if I was still trapped in the unsettling dream. Slowly, the familiar surroundings of the cottage came into focus.

I glanced down and let out a shaky breath. The manuscript pages were still covered in Eleanor's elegant script. The eerie events of the night must have been nothing more than a vivid nightmare.

Rubbing the fatigue from my eyes, I rose unsteadily to my feet. A dull ache had settled into my neck from sleeping hunched over. Wincing, I shuffled over to the bed and collapsed onto the cool sheets. My exhausted mind and body begged for rest, yet a nagging anxiety still gnawed at me.

As I stared up at the ceiling, the lingering unease from my nightmare clung to me like cobwebs. The dark corners of the cottage seemed to press in, shadows flickering in my peripheral vision. Closing my eyes tight, I tried to calm my jittery nerves.

"Just sleep," I whispered to myself. But as I drifted off, Eleanor's cryptic words from the manuscript echoed through my thoughts:

"Even in slumber, one cannot escape what lies in wait..."

———————

The morning sun cast a pale light through the gauzy curtains, doing little to warm the chill of the cottage. As I prepared my coffee, its rich scent failed to mask an underlying mustiness that seemed to seep from the very walls. Sipping cautiously, I turned to reach for the book I had left on the coffee table the night before, only to find it absent. A moment's search revealed it perched on a shelf across the room — an impossible migration that set my heart fluttering with unease.

I told myself it was a lapse in memory, nothing more. Yet, as I sat down once again to weave words into the fabric of Eleanor's unfinished tale, I could not ignore the sensation that the story was weaving itself into mine. The protagonist, much like myself, felt her sanctuary become alien, each familiar object now a stranger within her own home. My hand trembled as I gripped the pen, and I caught my reflection in the window — was that a flicker of movement behind me? No, merely a trick of the light, surely.

But tricks of the light did not move books, nor did they relocate my coffee mug to the kitchen counter when I had left it beside my manuscript. Small changes, perhaps, but like whispers in the darkness, they echoed loudly against the silence of solitude.

"Focus, Claire," I muttered, chiding my flighty nerves. Yet my voice sounded thin, feeble against the oppressive stillness of the cottage.

Night descended with a swift certainty, cloaking the world outside in impenetrable darkness. Sleep beckoned, a siren's call promising refuge from the day's unsettling oddities. But rest proved elusive; my dreams were haunted by shadows that breathed along the edges of consciousness, and I stirred to wakefulness with a start.

A loud thud, abrupt and jarring, shattered the silence. My heart lodged itself in my throat as I lay there, frozen, listening for any sign that what I heard was more than a figment of my imagination. When no further sound came, I summoned the courage to peel back the covers and investigate.

In the moonlit corridor leading to Eleanor's study, my footsteps seemed too loud, a staccato rhythm punctuating the eerie quiet. As I pushed open the door, a draft greeted me — a cold caress that raised gooseflesh on my arms.

Books strewn across the floor, their pages splayed open as if in mid-conversation. The desk drawer gaped, and its contents vomited onto the ground. This chaos, this violation of order, it was a language I could not decipher, yet its message was clear: You are not alone.

Eleanor's specter loomed in the corner of my eye, her piercing gaze dissecting my disbelief. "Rationalize this, Claire," she seemed to whisper, her voice tinged with a mocking severity. But there was no one there, only echoes and emptiness and the overpowering scent of old paper and secrets.

My breath came in short gasps, the air thick with the tangible presence of something unseen. For the first time, the comforting mantle of skepticism slipped from my shoulders, leaving me exposed to the chilling possibility that the horrors I wrote of were not confined to the realm of fiction.

I backed away slowly, my mind a tempest of fear and fascination. The cottage, Eleanor's final masterpiece, had ensnared me in its narrative — one I could neither control nor comprehend. With each heartbeat, the line between author and character, reality and nightmare, grew ever more indistinct.

I turned, my eyes drawn to the manuscript on the desk.

A shiver ran through me as I picked it up, the ink still fresh on the paper. It was as if Eleanor's hand had guided mine, her voice whispering in my ear. The words were mine, yet they were not. They were a reflection of the cottage, of Eleanor, of the unseen presence that now seemed to permeate every corner.

I returned to the manuscript with a feverish determination, the unease gnawing at my insides like an insidious parasite. The pen danced across the paper in a macabre waltz, weaving a tale of forbidden secrets and spectral whispers that mirrored the very essence of this cottage.

"Reveal yourself," I scrawled, words for my protagonist, yet a desperate plea to the shadowy corners of my own reality. My fingers trembled as they traced the lineage of darkness that ran through her fictional family's blood, a lineage that now seemed to bleed into the fibers of my being.

In the throes of creation, a hollow click interrupted the rhythm of my thoughts. My gaze fell upon the desk — Eleanor's altar of storytelling — and there, I found a compartment previously shrouded in obscurity. A hidden latch yielded to my touch, more compliant than I anticipated, revealing a trove of letters bound by time and secrecy.

With hesitant hands, I unfurled the yellowed pages. The ink faded, but the words spoken with an intensity that time could not diminish. Eleanor's script twisted and curled like the incantations she described, tales of communing with shadows and bargaining with entities beyond the mortal veil. Each sentence was a thread, pulling me deeper into her labyrinthine world of the occult.

My heartbeat stuttered as I read, the boundary between Eleanor's life and my fiction blurring until indistinguishable. With every line, the air grew heavier, and the dim light cast monstrous shapes upon the walls that breathed in synchrony with my quickened pulse.

"Is this your legacy, Eleanor?" I whispered, my voice a stranger's in the oppressive silence. "Are your phantoms merely waiting for me to take up the mantle?"

The room seemed to answer with a stillness so profound it roared in my ears. I looked up from the letters, the revelation of Eleanor's hidden life igniting a conflagration of fear and morbid curiosity within me. It was then, in that liminal space between doubt and belief, that a shadow flickered at the periphery of my vision — a distortion in the fabric of the room, a shape where no shape should be.

I froze, my breath caught in the icy grip of dread. Had my mind conjured this specter, or had Eleanor's arcane practices breached the confines of death? I dared not blink for fear of what might manifest in the moment of darkness behind closed lids.

A chill slithered down my spine, a silent omen that the horrors I penned were not mine alone to control. And as I sat there, ensnared in the tendrils of a story far greater and more terrifying than any I could hope to conceive, I understood with visceral clarity: the narrative of Eleanor Hargrave was far from over, and I was but a character in its unfolding.

CHAPTER 4

FRIGHTWRITTEN

The click-clack of my heels against the wooden floorboards filled Eleanor's study with a hollow echo, a staccato rhythm that matched the pounding of my heart. I paused, eyeing the creeping shadows that seemed to swell and recede in the corners of the room like darkened tides. They beckoned with crooked fingers, but I resisted their silent call, forcing myself into the worn leather chair behind the desk.

With trembling fingers, I unfurled my manuscript, the crisp rustle of paper slicing through the oppressive silence. The pen — Eleanor's old fountain pen — was cool and heavy in my hand, grounding me. As I began to etch words onto the blank page, each stroke was a defiant whisper against the dread that sought to strangle me. My anxiety, once a ravenous beast clawing at my insides, gradually grew tame under the spell of creation. The alchemy of writing transmuted fear into something almost like power.

My protagonist — no, my doppelganger on those pages — conducted her own investigation within the haunted walls of her ancestral home. With each clue she unearthed, I felt the pull of parallel curiosity. The narrative demanded authenticity; it hungered for the secrets Eleanor had left behind.

I rose, my quest momentarily overriding the unease that clung to me like a second skin. Through the dimly lit corridors of the cottage, I moved with purpose, tracing the lines of Eleanor's life as if they were ley lines on a map of the arcane. Dust-coated trinkets and faded photographs whispered half-truths, each one a piece of the puzzle that was Eleanor Hargrave.

Back at the desk, the line between fact and fiction blurred like ink in water. I wove Eleanor's history into the fabric of the tale, stitching reality with strands of imagined horrors. Each revelation from the past seeped into my narrative, staining it with the hues of truth — or what passed for truth in this shrouded, shifting place.

The rhythm of this back-and-forth dance — the search and the scribe — became my incantation against the encroaching darkness. Yet even as I crafted this story of spectral hauntings and unspeakable fears, I could not shake the sense that something unseen watched, waited, and perhaps...even guided my hand.

I had not noticed the chill until a shiver coursed through my spine, as unwelcome and sharp as the scratch of a pen on paper. The room, once stifling with the midday heat, now bore an unnatural cold that seemed to seep from the very walls, enveloping me in its icy grip. I could see my breath, a ghostly vapor in the air, unfurling like the tendrils of a specter reaching forth from the nether.

Objects around me stirred — a pen rolled off the desk with a clatter, papers fluttered as if caught in a silent tempest, and books thudded to the floor of their own accord. My heart raced, matching the frenetic dance of those items possessed by unseen hands. Yet, amidst the chaos, a strange compulsion anchored me to my seat. The manuscript before me was alive, each word a pulse in the veins of its mystery.

"Who are you?" I whispered to the empty room, half-expecting an answer from the shadows that seemed to watch with intent.

Then, as I carved out a scene where my protagonist

faced a reflection that was not her own, I felt the line between my world and the one I created fray to near invisibility. I wrote of a mirror, tarnished by time, revealing a figure draped in mourning — and when I dared lift my gaze from the page, my eyes met the very same visage within the study's ancient glass.

The figure in the mirror mimicked my stillness, its presence a pale imitation of life. A scream lodged itself in my throat, muffled only by disbelief. In my haste to retreat, the chair beneath me crashed to the floor, a sound swallowed immediately by the silence that resumed its oppressive reign.

"Impossible," I muttered, though my voice betrayed the uncertainty that clawed at the edges of my conviction. With trepidation, I approached the mirror, my flesh crawling at the prospect of confronting this blurred reality. My fingers brushed against the cool surface, half expecting them to sink into another realm. They did not, yet the figure remained, watching me with eyes hollowed by sorrow — or was it accusation?

"Are you a phantom of my creation?" The question hung in the air, unanswered, the echo of my own voice a mockery of the solace I sought. The figure gave no sign, and I was left to wonder whether my mind had woven such a convincing tapestry of horror that it had come to life or if Eleanor's legacy was truly reaching beyond the grave to ensnare me in its tragic past.

Each breath I drew was laden with the weight of dread, and I knew then that the manuscript and I were bound together by more than mere ink. It was a covenant written in whispers and sealed with the shadows that lingered in my periphery — those that shifted and murmured with the secrets of the dead.

As I sat there, the first light of dawn crept through the

gaps in the curtains, casting a spectral glow over the chaos that encircled me. My fingers, stiff from hours of frantic scribbling and sorting, fumbled with the papers scattered like autumn leaves across the floor — my writing, Eleanor's cryptic letters, fragments of the original manuscript that seemed to bleed into my reality.

I blinked away the sting of red-rimmed eyes, the remnants of sleepless nights clinging to me like cobwebs. With each document I pinned to the corkboard, my mind wove together a tapestry darker than the one that shrouded the cottage outside. Eleanor's past, my present experiences, and the twisting narrative of the manuscript converged into a labyrinthine web, each thread pulsing with unspoken secrets.

The silence of the room was a vast ocean, and I, a solitary vessel adrift upon its tides, charting a course through the murky depths of memory and imagination. The board before me bore witness to this journey, an arcane map marked by lines and notes that sketched out the contours of an enigma far more complex than I had ever fathomed.

With every connection I made, the shadows seemed to lean in closer, as if drawn by the gravity of revelation. Yet fear, that constant companion that whispered lies in the quiet moments, found no purchase in the steel resolve that now armored my heart.

I stepped back, my breath a mist that mingled with the dust motes dancing in the slanting rays of the sun. The board was a mosaic of madness and truth, a challenge issued by the dead to the living. I could not turn away; the story called to me, a siren song woven from the very fabric of my soul.

"Let the ghosts of this house bear witness," I whispered, my voice a blade slicing through the veil of uncertainty. "I will uncover what lurks within these walls."

Taking up my pen — a talisman against the darkness

— I seated myself once again at the desk. The ink flowed like blood from a wound, each word a step deeper into the heart of the maze. There was no turning back. The mystery of Eleanor, the essence of the tale that bound us, pulsed beneath my skin, demanding to be laid bare.

I wrote with a fervor born of desperation, the rhythm of my sentences a drumbeat marching towards some inevitable conclusion. The cottage, with its creaking bones and sighing winds, watched over me — an altar to the unknown where I offered up my resolve.

For in the pursuit of truth, I knew there would be a cost, a price to be paid in flesh and spirit. But I was prepared to pay it, to chase the whispering specters to the very edges of reason and beyond, until the story revealed itself, whole and terrible, upon the page. And so, with the morning light as my witness, I surrendered to the haunting embrace of the words, letting them lead me wherever they may.

CHAPTER 5

FRIGHTWRITTEN

The wheel felt cold and real under my fingertips, a stark contrast to the spectral shadows that had begun to take up residence in my peripheral vision. Sleep had become an elusive wraith, taunting me with its absence. The road to town unfurled like a ribbon through the mist, and I was drawn inexorably towards the heart of my dread.

I parked hastily by the museum — a quaint reminder of the town's love for its own history — and hurried inside, feeling oddly exposed. Timothy Ward, the keeper of local legends, stood amidst relics of the past, his presence as dependable as the books that filled his domain.

"Timothy," I said, trying to keep my voice steady. "I need to know about Eleanor Hargrave."

His welcoming smile faded as he took in my flustered state. "Claire," he said, pushing his glasses back up his nose, "what's got you so worked up?"

I couldn't tell if he was worried or wary, but either way, his reaction did nothing to calm my nerves.

"It's her story," I explained, my words tumbling out. "Something's not right about it."

Timothy led me to his office, a catacomb of ancient tomes and artifacts that seemed to breathe with memories of their own. His words rose and fell in a measured cadence, his voice barely above a whisper in the hushed sanctuary of history.

"Eleanor's tale is one of brilliance shadowed by

madness," he confessed, and I listened, transfixed, as the room seemed to close in around us.

Timothy leaned back in his chair, a faraway look in his eyes as he recounted Eleanor's tale.

"She was a literary star from the start — her first novel rocketed up the bestseller charts when she was just 25. The critics adored her vivid imagination and haunting prose. Her books were devoured by adoring fans across the country. For a decade, she was the undisputed queen of horror fiction."

He paused, removing his glasses to rub at tired eyes. "But over time, something changed. With each new book, she withdrew more and more from the limelight. She stopped doing book tours, interviews, public appearances — it was like she wanted to fade into obscurity."

I leaned forward, hanging on his every word. Outside, the wind howled mournfully around the eaves of the archives building.

"Rumors started to swirl about her increasingly eccentric behavior. Some said she had turned to the occult — holding séances and communing with spirits. Others whispered of bizarre rituals and ceremonies held at her isolated cottage. But no one knew for sure what she was seeking through these dark practices."

Timothy's gaze grew distant again. "In the end, I believe she delved too greedily and too deep into forces beyond her understanding. She became obsessed with summoning something...some arcane entity or ancient power. All her talent and knowledge were bent towards this single purpose."

He shook his head sadly. "It consumed her, body and soul. Whatever she had unearthed ultimately proved to be her undoing."

A log collapsed in the fireplace, making me jump. Outside, the wind continued its mournful keening as if in lamentation for Eleanor's doomed quest. I sat in silence as Timothy's words sank in.

"Found dead at her desk," Timothy murmured, his voice a ghostly echo in the chamber of secrets.

The image of Eleanor — stiff, her blue eyes vacant and staring at nothing, the manuscript, an unholy relic, lying incomplete before her — seared itself into my mind. My heart hammered against my ribcage, each beat a knell tolling for the folly of my own ambition.

"Is that how I will end, too?" The question slipped from my lips, unbidden, as the specter of my future painted itself in grim strokes upon the canvas of Eleanor's past.

Timothy's words slithered through the air, a serpent coiling tighter with each revelation. "Tread carefully, Claire. Eleanor...she was delving into something far beyond the realm of a simple ghost story," he said, his eyes darting to the door as if fearing the very mention might invite unwelcome spirits.

"An incantation, perhaps?" I ventured, my voice barely a whisper, but it was as if I'd struck a dissonant chord on an ancient piano, one that reverberated through the bones of the building.

"Possibly," Timothy admitted, his voice trembling. "The manuscript — her final work — it was rumored to be more than mere fiction. An unfinished ritual."

A wave of realization crashed over me, leaving me breathless and shaken. I remembered the nights spent hunched over her manuscript, the ink flowing from my pen not just onto paper but seeping into the very fabric of my reality. Memories flooded back — shadows lingering at the edges of my vision, growing darker with every word I transcribed, every sentence I wove from the whispers that echoed in the recesses of my mind.

The color drained from my face as the true nature of what I'd been nurturing unfolded before me. It was not simply a story; it was a curse, a half-completed invocation that I had been blindly, foolishly bringing to life.

"What have I done?" I whispered, my voice barely audible. But there was no comfort to be found for a writer who had played with fire only to find herself engulfed by the flames.

The drive back to the cottage was a descent into madness. The car radio crackled to life of its own accord, static-laced whispers slithering through the speakers, forming words that remained just outside my grasp. Shadows clung to the vehicle, flitting across the windshield, dark figures that chased me down the winding roads.

Upon arriving, the world tilted. The study door swung open before I could touch it, greeting me with a maelstrom of swirling pages. Manuscript leaves danced in a spectral wind that defied the stillness of the air. And there, amidst the chaos of fluttering paper, it took shape — a form darker than the void between stars, a malevolent spirit that writhed and twisted as though it were made of smoke and sin.

It was the first time I saw it clearly: a grotesque parody of human form, born from the abyss of Eleanor's unspoken words and my own unwitting conjuration. Its eyes glowed like embers, searing into my soul, a silent accusation of the horror I had wrought.

"Is this what you wanted, Claire?" it seemed to hiss, a question that bore the weight of a thousand sleepless nights, a thousand doubts whispered to the silence of an uncaring universe.

I stood rooted to the spot, the breath stolen from my lungs, the terror of realization gripping me with a ferocity that threatened to tear me apart from within. This was the legacy of Eleanor Hargrave, the inheritance I had claimed with eager, ignorant hands. This was the price of ambition, paid in full by the currency of nightmares.

Papers levitated around me, a carousel of cursed words spinning in a room that had become the heart of my own personal nightmare. The spirit reached out with tendrils of shadow, each one a whisper of temptation and terror. It was calling to me, luring me closer with the sibilant promise of dark wonders and forbidden knowledge.

I could feel it inside my head, a presence as invasive as it was insidious. It toyed with my deepest insecurities, the fears that I had cloaked in layers of ambition and pride. "Claire," it seemed to murmur, using my name like a weapon, "isn't this the greatness you sought?"

The pen lay on my desk, an innocuous instrument transformed into a conductor of chaos. I could leave it, abandon this madness to save myself from a fate I was only beginning to comprehend. Or I could embrace the power that surged through every line of Eleanor's accursed manuscript and mine.

In the throes of my internal struggle, it was not courage that moved my hand but a desperation born of years of grappling with mediocrity. I was Claire Monroe, the woman who yearned to transcend the ordinary, to etch her name upon the annals of literary legend. And so, with trembling fingers, I seized the pen.

The moment the nib touched the paper, it was as if I had struck a deal with the devil himself. Ink flowed, winding across the blank page like a serpent — a physical manifestation of my inner turmoil. I wrote not just words but incantations, each syllable strengthening the spirit's hold on our world.

It grew more corporeal with every stroke, its form solidifying into something grotesquely humanoid. It was a horror made flesh by my own hand, a twisted muse spun from the loom of my darkest aspirations.

And yet, I could not stop. The dance of creation was too intoxicating. As the pen scratched onward, the whispers grew louder, the shadows darker, the air heavier with the scent of impending doom. The spirit's ember eyes burned brighter, watching me with a gaze that knew no mercy, only hunger — for fear, for life, for art.

With the final word of the passage, I paused, breath ragged, and dared to look up. My reflection in the windowpane was a ghastly caricature of the writer I once was: eyes wide with the realization of what I had summoned, yet ablaze with the feverish resolve to finish what I had started.

"See it through," the spirit seemed to hiss, its voice now clear and commanding. "See it through, Claire, and be remembered."

I would see it through, I decided then, in the haunted quiet of the study. The legacy of Eleanor Hargrave would be mine to bear, a yoke fashioned by both curse and creation. And though horror gripped my heart, it was entwined with a determination as unyielding as the grave.

CHAPTER 6

FRIGHTWRITTEN

I sat amidst the ruins of my own making, the cottage a reflection of the tumult within my mind. My hand moved feverishly across the page as if possessed by a will beyond my own. A vase shattered against the wall, its fragments waltzing to the floor in a cruel pirouette of destruction. I flinched, a mere tremor passing through me, but I could not — would not — halt the flow of ink that bled from my pen.

The disarray around me was a silent scream, a physical echo of the narrative chaos that spilled from my quivering hand. The overturned chair lay like a fallen comrade; the cracked windows, like fractured realities, let in a howling wind that carried whispers of the damned. With every word I etched into the parchment, the barrier between the tale and this world thinned until whispers became wails and shadows took form.

A chill caressed the nape of my neck. A lover's touch turned sinister as the air grew thick with the scent of dread. I knew I should stop, I knew, yet the story demanded its due — a pound of flesh from the depths of my psyche.

And then, without warning, I was no longer the architect of horror but its captive audience. The room flickered, and I found myself standing in the corridor of the house I had conjured — a hall of endless doors and creeping darkness. My heart pounded a relentless rhythm, each beat a knell that echoed off the oppressive walls.

I ran, the hem of my sweater catching on unseen

splinters, the sound of my breath harsh against the silence. Shadowy figures pursued me, their forms nebulous but intent malevolent. They were born of my imagination, yet here they hunted me, hungry for the life I had inadvertently breathed into them.

With every rapid transition, the desk, the manuscript, the corridors, my reality frayed at the edges. It was a tapestry unraveling, threads of reason slipping through my desperate grasp. I was Claire Monroe, the writer, the creator, the destroyer — but who was I within the pages of my own tragedy?

Time looped upon itself, a serpent swallowing its tail. At one moment, I was hunched over the manuscript, the next fleeing down the infinite passage of my fears. My sanctuary had become my cell, my words, the bars that held me captive.

"Finish it," a voice whispered, as ethereal as the specters that stalked me. "Complete the tale, Claire."

But what ending could there be when the line between fiction and the flesh had all but vanished? What hope did I have when the ghosts of my mind walked the same floors as I did? Every sentence I wrote, every paragraph I completed, drew me deeper into this waking nightmare — a nightmare of my own design, one I could neither wake from nor escape.

The air in the cottage grew colder, a creeping chill that slithered along my spine. I paused, my hand trembling above the manuscript, the ink on my pen a pool of night waiting to spill its secrets upon the page. There was a silence — a suffocating absence of sound that clawed at the edges of my sanity. I dared not breathe, for in that stillness, something stirred.

My gaze lifted, drawn inexorably to the mirror perched atop the mantel. The reflection was no longer my own. Obsidian eyes, hollow with malice, bore into mine from the glass. A figure, dark and distorted, took shape behind me; its form writhed like smoke caught in a tempest. Each word I had written lent substance to this specter, each sentence a chain binding it to my reality.

With a start, I turned but found nothing — no presence save for the lingering dread that embraced me. Yet the mirror betrayed the truth: there it stood, its hand outstretched as if to pluck the very soul from my chest. A gasp escaped my lips, a silent prayer that went unanswered in the gloom of my self-made purgatory.

No more could I deny the horror I had conjured. This spirit, this entity born of ink and imagination, craved existence beyond the parchment. It hungered for the warmth of life, and I, in my folly, had laid out the feast.

Panic, sharp and unrelenting, spurred me into motion. I lurched toward the door, desperate to escape the confines of this haunted abode. But the cottage, once my haven, had other designs. It shuddered as though sharing in the malevolence of its unseen occupant. An invisible force struck me, throwing me backward with such violence that my breath was stolen. I crumpled to the floor, the taste of iron blooming in my mouth.

"Open!" I cried, staggering to my feet, but the door mocked my efforts, sealed shut by an unseen will. I turned to the windows, my hands clawing at the latches, but the panes resisted my touch as if forged from the very fabric of night. They would not yield, would not fracture, no matter the desperation of my blows.

Trapped. The realization was a vise around my heart, squeezing until I thought it might burst. My sanctuary had betrayed me, the walls pressing in with quiet malevolence. The spirit I had birthed through my words now held dominion over this place, and I was the unwelcome guest in its newly claimed realm.

I retreated from the relentless barriers, my back pressing against the wooden walls. The weight of my ambition, my creative yearning, bore down upon me with the gravity of gravestones. I had sought to craft a world within my pages, never dreaming that it might seek to craft me in return.

The cottage, once filled with the whispers of inspiration, now echoed with the laughter of shadows. And somewhere within that cacophony of darkness, I found the truth: I was the architect of my own damnation, the writer who had penned her way into a prison of her own making.

With every shallow breath, the specter drew nearer, its presence a malignant promise that clung to me like the chill of the grave. There, amidst the wreckage of my ambitions, I awaited the next chapter — the one I would be compelled to write or the one that would be written for me.

The corners of the study whispered with a madness that was not entirely my own. I had become little more than a vessel, a conduit for the horror I had unwittingly invited into this world through the fervor of my pen. There, in that dim corner where light dared not linger, I sat huddled; my fingers white-knuckled as they gripped the manuscript — the tome of my downfall.

The dark figure — it was no mere wraith now but a looming specter of ink and malevolence — stood over me with an oppressiveness that suffocated the very air. Its once formless shape had found substance in the terror of my own making, its eyes glowing like coals set to ignite the tinder of reality itself.

"Write," it commanded, a whisper that slithered into my ears and coiled around my mind. The voice was at once ancient and immediate, a chilling caress from a time when darkness reigned unchallenged.

I raised my trembling hand, the pen slick between my

sweat-drenched fingers. There was no escaping the conclusion that had been set into motion by my own insatiable curiosity, my reckless pursuit of literary achievement. How trivial those ambitions seemed now, how bitterly ironic that my quest for a legacy would anchor me to a tale of perpetual horror.

A single tear breached the dam of my composure, trailing down my cheek as I touched the pen to the paper. A drop of ink fell — a harbinger of doom that spread across the page, seeping into the fibers like poison through veins.

"Finish your story, Claire Monroe," the spirit intoned, its voice echoing the darkest recesses of my fraught psyche. "And know that with each word, you are binding yourself ever tighter to this fate."

The utter defeat in my gaze reflected the monstrosity of what I'd become: a writer enslaved by her own creation, a puppet enacting a narrative that strangled my soul. The rhythm of my heartbeat faltered, keeping time with the dread that pulsed through the room.

In that moment, the cottage — and indeed, the world beyond — ceased to exist. There was only the manuscript, the pen, and the unyielding gaze of the dark figure that held dominion over both. As I surrendered to the inexorable pull of the story that demanded to be told, the walls of reality crumbled, leaving nothing but the echo of my pen scratching against the parchment, chronicling the twilight of my sanity.

CHAPTER 7

FRIGHTWRITTEN

I heard her before I felt the cold, a whisper threading through the oppressive silence of the room. My breath fogged in the air, and a chill crept up my spine as pale light spilled across Eleanor's writing desk, casting long shadows that danced like specters on the walls.

"Eleanor?" My voice was a mere wisp, disbelief painting each syllable.

"Dear child," came the soft reply, echoing from a world not quite our own. She materialized before me, translucent and serene, her silver hair aglow with otherworldly luminescence. "You must finish what I could not."

The ghost of Eleanor Hargrave, once a reclusive scribe of nightmarish tales, now stood as my reluctant beacon in the encroaching darkness. The room seemed to contract around us, the walls inching closer, eager to listen.

"Trapped within the story...it is the only way." Her voice carried an urgency that pierced my heart with equal parts terror and resolve. Her spectral form flickered like the last desperate gasp of a dying candle.

I understood then with a clarity that shattered my lingering doubts. The manuscript, the cursed narrative that had haunted me since I first set foot in this forsaken cottage, held the key to salvation — or damnation.

"Rewrite the ending, Claire," she implored, her image dissolving into the cold air, leaving behind the echo of her command.

I stood up, my limbs heavy as if weighed down by an invisible force. The darkness seemed alive, its presence oppressive. Whispers slithered through the shadows, like tendrils of ink seeking to ensnare me.

"Get out of my head," I muttered, more to steady myself than anything else. Summoning what courage I had left, I stumbled toward the desk, arm outstretched. Doubt gnawed at me, but desperation drove me forward.

My fingers closed around the pen, which suddenly glowed with an otherworldly light reminiscent of Eleanor's spectral form. It pulsed with potential, with her essence, like a lifeline thrown across the divide between worlds.

Taking a shaky breath, I pressed the pen to paper. The nib grazed the surface with a strange intimacy. Words flowed, a stream of hope and horror, each letter a stand against the encroaching darkness that threatened both my story and my sanity.

"This ends now," I said under my breath, the ink binding the spirit to my will, to the tale that would become its prison. I wrote with a frantic energy, driven by fear and an unyielding need to reclaim control of my own narrative.

And so, with Eleanor's whispered guidance fading into memory and the dark adversary pressing close, I penned the words that would either doom or deliver me.

Ink spread across the parchment, dark and ominous, as I fought against the supernatural force that had invaded Eleanor's sanctuary. I wrote frantically, but the words twisted before my eyes — letters warping, sentences unraveling into gibberish under some malevolent influence. The air felt heavy, tainted with an unseen menace.

"Come on, not now," I muttered, furiously crossing out the garbled text and rewriting what I meant to say. Each word was a small victory, a pushback against the darkness that seemed intent on derailing my efforts.

I stood up from the desk, my hands shaking. This was getting out of control. I had to do something drastic to stop this before it was too late.

In a panic, I decided to burn the manuscript to stop this madness. I gathered up all the pages, crumpling them in my fists, and brought them to the small metal trash can in the corner of the study. Taking a match, I lit the corners of the pages, dropping them into the can. Flames licked at the paper, curling the edges.

As I watched the pages turn to ash, a feeling of relief washed over me. It was finally over. The spirit's hold on me was broken.

But then I heard it. The scratching of a pen on paper. Spinning around, I saw in horror that the manuscript lay intact on the desk. Even as the last embers burned down in the trash can, the words scrawled themselves across the pages as if written by an invisible hand.

I rushed to the desk, grabbing the papers, but they would not tear. I could not burn them or, in any other way, destroy them. The manuscript simply reappeared, whole and unblemished.

Collapsing into the desk chair, I stared at the pages in resigned despair. I was trapped — the spirit would never let me go. Not until I finished the story on its terms.

The room descended into chaos: papers whirled through the air like a blizzard of forgotten stories. In the center of this storm, I stood my ground, pen scratching across the page with desperate determination.

But the battle wasn't just around me — it was inside me, too. Shadows gathered, taking on a familiar shape. My own face, distorted by doubt and fear, seemed to stare back at me from every corner, giving voice to all the insecurities I'd tried to ignore.

"Failure," one shadow taunted, its voice a serrated whisper.

"Mediocre," another sneered, a specter of scorn.

"Never enough," they chanted, a litany of despair.

I stumbled, a word faltering, ink splattering like a wound upon the page. But then, from the depths of my mind, Eleanor's success bloomed — a beacon in the gloom. Her stern countenance, those piercing blue eyes that had seen through veils and beyond worlds, bolstered my resolve.

"Silence," I commanded, my voice gaining strength. With each conquered doubt, the pen surged forward, the narrative unfurling beneath my command. Memories of Eleanor's triumphs lent vigor to my strokes, her literary prowess now a mantle I donned with fierce pride.

"Your time is ending," I whispered to the darkness, both within and without, and the shadows trembled.

The entity redoubled its efforts, an unseen tempest battering against the bulwark of my will. It sought to drown me in the abyss of my own creation, but I was no longer the timid soul it presumed to devour. I was Claire Monroe, heir to Hargrave's legacy, mistress of tales that could chill the very marrow. And I would not be undone.

So I wrote, and the world trembled.

The spirit's icy tendrils coiled around my wrist, seeking to still my pen. I shook them off with a snarl. The manuscript before me warped, letters rearranging themselves into monstrous shapes. I ripped the tainted pages away, starting anew. Windows shattered, shards raining down like crystalline tears. The walls groaned, buckling under some unfathomable force.

Still, I wrote on, weaving the threads of the story with frantic fingers. I would not relent, could not relent until the final sentence was etched upon the page. This was my purpose, my birthright — to spin nightmares made real with ink and pen. To conquer the ancient evil with the timeless magic of narrative.

Yet even as the words flowed from my pen, I sensed a sinister shift. The letters on the page seemed to crawl and contort before my eyes. My elegant script warped into a jagged, erratic scrawl. The spirit was rewriting my narrative, infusing its malevolence into every line.

I fought to regain control, gripping the pen with white-knuckled intensity. But the more I struggled, the further the tale diverged from my intent. The protagonist transformed into a wretched, broken soul ripe for the fiend's corruption. Shadowy tendrils crept from the margins, poised to drag the heroine into their stygian depths.

This was the spirit's realm now, a nightmare of my own making. I could only watch, helpless, as it twisted my story into a gnarled mockery of truth. Yet even in the face of defeat, a glimmer of hope remained. Eleanor's stern voice echoed in my mind: "All darkness must pass. Dawn comes, inevitably."

The spirit's insidious influence spread through every line, poisoning my tale from within. I tore at the tainted pages in anguish, but the corruption ran deeper than mere paper and ink. This was a battle for the soul of the story itself.

My protagonist, once bold and defiant, was reduced to a hollow shell, empty eyes staring blankly from a gaunt face. Her world decayed around her in a haze of nightmare logic — stairs leading nowhere, familiar rooms distorted into Escheresque impossibilities. She stumbled onward, hopeless, only a puppet dancing on tangled strings.

I grabbed the pen again in a white-knuckled grip, determined to excise this cancerous plot tumor. But my hand moved as if possessed, scribbling scenes of depravity I could never have imagined. The spirit exulted in my horror, feeding on anguish as I watched helplessly.

Then, in the darkest hour, Eleanor's words returned to me once more. Her voice rang out, clear above that abyssal din:

"Every story must contain both darkness and light. Do not fear the shadows, child — they make the dawn all the sweeter."

Of course. To banish evil, I must turn to the light. My protagonist needed hope to fight against despair.

CHAPTER 8

FRIGHTWRITTEN

The room grew cold, a creeping chill that slithered beneath my skin and coiled around my spine. Shadows lengthened across the study, drawn out by an unseen hand as if the very light was being devoured. I felt it then — the presence of the entity, no longer content to lurk in the periphery of my vision. It manifested before me, its true form, a nightmare born from the abyss.

"Can you see me, Claire?" it whispered, its voice a symphony of hushed tones that swirled together into a chilling melody. The darkness coalesced into a writhing mass, tendrils of blackness reaching out like the arms of the damned. Within the seething void, eyes glowed like dying embers, fixating on me with a hunger that was palpable. My hand trembled, gripping the pen, which suddenly felt feeble, a laughable defense against this ancient monstrosity.

"Once, authors sought me out," it murmured, and I could hear the echoes of countless voices stolen over generations. "They longed for inspiration, for the words that would grant them immortality. And I fed upon their craving, their spirits ink within my veins."

I swallowed hard, my throat tight with fear, even as I squared my shoulders and held my ground. This creature, this devourer of creativity, had chosen me as its next victim. But I would not yield so easily.

"Look upon me, Claire," the spirit continued, sensing the steel in my resolve. Its grotesque figure began to melt away, shifting like smoke on the wind. In its place, visions unfurled — glittering and seductive. Bestselling novels bearing my name, crowds chanting for the woman who'd penned worlds into existence, prestigious awards bestowed with reverent hands. My heart quickened at the sight, and for a fleeting moment, I allowed myself to be ensnared by the dream.

"Such glory can be yours," it cooed, its whispers now dipped in honey, a stark contrast to the terror it had first inspired. "All I ask is for you to embrace me. Surrender to my embrace, and your name shall be etched across history."

I faltered, my pen — a symbol of my struggle, my dreams — lowering ever so slightly. The temptation was exquisite, a siren's call promising everything my soul yearned for. Yet, deep within the recesses of my mind, where doubt liked to fester and bloom, a voice cautioned me. The price of such a bargain would surely be more than I could bear.

"Your fears are the nectar from which I draw life," it said, its voice a gentle lullaby now. "Feed me your anxieties, your insecurities. Let them be the foundation of our covenant."

In the quiet of that haunted study, surrounded by the phantoms of promised fame, I stood at the precipice of a choice that would define not only my future but the essence of my being. Would I surrender to the darkness for a fleeting taste of greatness? Or would I resist, forging my path through the unknown?

"Decide, Claire," the spirit urged, its tendrils of temptation caressing the edges of my consciousness. "Embrace your destiny with me, or languish in obscurity."

A battle waged within me, ambition clashing with apprehension, each vying for dominion over my soul. Time seemed to stand still, the oppressive silence punctuated only by the whispering entreaties of the shadowed fiend before me. And in that moment of wavering will, I realized the true weight of my decision, the gravity of the crossroads at which I now stood.

A spectral chill brushed my shoulder, and I knew without turning that Eleanor had returned. No words passed between us; her silence spoke volumes about all she had endured. Instead, a ghostly touch suffused me with visions: the ethereal strands of Eleanor's life, woven through time like silver threads in a dark tapestry.

I witnessed her solitary days, her hand racing across pages in a desperate attempt to outpace the encroaching darkness. Her nights were battles waged with only the soft glow of the desk lamp as her ally, the scratch of her pen a constant rhythm in the quiet. And then, the culmination of her struggle — facing the entity, an indomitable force that demanded everything.

With each memory that seared into my mind, I saw not triumphs but pyrrhic victories etched with sorrow. It became clear — the spirit's promises were fool's gold, their luster masking an insidious corruption. My resolve solidified like ice in my veins, and the pen in my hand was now my chosen weapon.

"Thank you, Eleanor," I whispered, a silent vow to honor her legacy.

The pen flew across the page, my mind racing to stay ahead of its furious pace. Words poured forth in a torrent, rising from some deep wellspring of creative power I had never before tapped. I no longer questioned or doubted — I simply let the narrative flow through me, the story writing itself in a dizzying cascade of imagery and emotion.

With each paragraph, the spirit's presence seemed to grow heavier, pressing down on me with suffocating intensity. Strange visions swam before my eyes — phantom landscapes, monstrous shapes, glyphs in ancient tongues — all rising unbidden from the realm I was crafting with such perilous speed. I could feel the entity twining itself around my thoughts, insinuating its inky being into the fibers of the tale.

And yet, I could not stop. The same fervent energy that fed the spirit also filled me with reckless abandon. I was drunk on words, intoxicated by the perilous precipice on which I teetered. All was laid bare before my inner eye — light and darkness, hope and despair, dream and nightmare. I poured it all onto the page in a literary libation, heedless of what might slip through along with it...

And then came inspiration in the form of my aunt, Eleanor. Her Gothic tales enthralled me as a child. Now, her mentorship emboldened me to embrace the darkness and transform it into art. Little did I know what her wisdom would unleash. But from that darkness came the light of revelation.

I was a writer. Creating stories was my purpose, my legacy. The entity had tried to corrupt that gift, but ultimately, it made me stronger. I knew I had found my way home. The pen continued to dance across the paper as if possessed, each stroke igniting the ink into luminescent words that crackled with arcane energy. The study warped around me, reality fraying at the edges as my narrative took hold.

"Let this be your unmaking," I declared, voice steadier than my shaking hands.

The spirit howled, a sound that was not of this Earth, its form contorting in an agonized ballet. Words became chains, sentences formed cages, and paragraphs constructed a prison that no amount of cunning could evade. As I wrote, I was rewriting more than just the story — I was altering the fabric that bound the entity to our world.

It thrashed within the confines of my tale, tendrils

dissolving like smoke in the wind, eyes dimming from a nefarious glow to feeble embers. Each sentence I crafted was a nail in the coffin of this nightmare, each paragraph a seal on its fate.

"Your reign ends here," I intoned, the final words pouring from my soul as much as from my pen. "In this story, you are powerless."

And with every ounce of conviction bleeding through the ink, I felt the weight of history, the countless souls that had been ensnared before me, bearing witness to my resistance. I would not succumb to the same shadows that had claimed them.

The entity's scream, once a symphony of despair, dwindled to a desperate whisper as it unraveled before my eyes. I had become the author of its undoing, a scribe of salvation for those it sought to devour. Through my words, I was free.

I scrawled the final sentence, my hand driven by a force that surged through me, fierce and unyielding. The pen's nib scratched the paper sharply as I finished, and in that instant, the very air seemed to shiver with anticipation. A light erupted around me, its brilliance outshining the candles that had long since guttered into oblivion and then — darkness.

Silence fell like a curtain, heavy and absolute. My chest heaved with each breath, my lungs desperate for air after the suffocating grip of terror. Slowly, I opened my eyes. The spirit was no more, its presence erased as if it had been nothing but a figment of some fevered nightmare. All that remained was the manuscript, innocuous on the desk, its pages still whispering of ink freshly spilled.

Rising from the chair, I felt different, as though I had shed an old skin, brittle with doubts and fears. My reflection in the windowpane told of this transformation; there was a certainty in my gaze, a solidity to my stance that had been absent when I first crossed the threshold into Eleanor's world. The study bathed in the blush of dawn, the early light casting a soft glow over everything it touched.

With tentative fingers, I reached for the manuscript. It was warm, almost pulsing with a life all its own. I did not recoil. Instead, I cradled it, feeling the thrum of words that had conjured salvation. There was respect, yes, but also a profound understanding that bloomed within me — these words were power, they were deliverance.

As I turned toward the door, the weight of the manuscript in my hands rendered me grounded and present. My shadow stretched out before me, elongated and strangely comforting. But in the moment before I stepped beyond the room's embrace, the shape of my silhouette morphed. It took on the form of another — tall, poised, the unmistakable outline of Eleanor Hargrave.

The echo of her legacy was etched into the walls of that place, into the very air that hung charged with the remnants of our battle. I had walked in her footsteps, and now, I carried her story alongside my own. Our tales intertwined, written in the language of loss and defiance.

Leaving the study behind, I moved through the cottage with a silent reverence. As the door closed behind me, sealing the room and its memories away, I knew that the whispers of what transpired would linger, haunting the space between the lines of my own narrative.

But fear was no longer my companion. I had looked into the abyss and, through words, wrenched myself from its depths. The path forward was mine to write, and in the quiet of the morning, with the manuscript under my arm and Eleanor's indomitable spirit at my back, I began anew.

———

I loaded the last box into my car and took one final look at the cottage that had been both my home and prison for the past few months. An uneasiness settled deep in my bones — something was still very wrong with that house. It had taken a piece of my soul that I would never reclaim. As I glanced up at the attic window, a shiver coursed through me. Though I'd won a personal victory against the entity, it was back, glaring at me through the curtains. I knew, without question, I would never set foot in that house again.

As I slid into the driver's seat and turned the ignition, a cold wind whipped through the trees, rattling the windows. I peered into the rearview mirror, half expecting to see Eleanor's ghostly form watching me from the porch. But there was only the "For Sale" sign rocking violently in the overgrown yard.

"Good riddance," I muttered, peeling away from the property without a backwards glance. The further I drove, the lighter I felt, as if a physical weight was lifting from my shoulders. By the time I reached the rural highway, the sun breaking through the clouds, I realized I was crying. Tears of relief, of grief, of hope.

I had miles yet to go, a new story waiting to be written. But I was alive, and for now, that was enough. Eleanor's legacy would not be forgotten, but it was no longer mine to bear alone. We had forged something powerful in the darkness, something that lived inside me now, fortifying the words I still had left to give.

This was not the ending either of us would have chosen. But it was the one I would write nonetheless.

MALATHOR'S WELL

ERIK
SHEIN

MELISSA
DAVIS

KAREN
FULLER

CHAPTER 1
MALATHOR'S WELL

The ancient well whispered its first secret as the Porters arrived: it had been waiting for them.

The Porters' battered station wagon limped up the overgrown driveway, its engine wheezing like a dying beast as it approached their new start. There, looming before them, stood the old house—a decrepit two-story Victorian that seemed to watch their approach with hollow, shadowed eyes. Its steeply pitched roof, crowned with slate tiles missing in places like gaps in a mouthful of rotting teeth, cast long shadows across the weed-choked lawn. As the car's headlights swept across the façade, they illuminated a turret rising from the right corner, its conical roof slightly askew, giving the unsettling impression of a crooked witch's hat perched atop the structure. The station wagon shuddered to a halt, and in the sudden silence, the house's presence felt overwhelming—a silent sentinel holding its breath, waiting to exhale secrets long buried within its walls.

The front porch stretched the width of the house, its wooden boards warped and creaking, promising to betray any step with a mournful groan. Ornate balusters, their white paint chipped and flaking, lined the porch like a row of weathered guardians. The porch roof sagged slightly, supported by columns that twisted ever so subtly as if trying to writhe free from their burden.

Windows, tall and narrow, peppered the façade, their panes reflecting the encroaching forest with an eerie distortion. The attic window, a perfect half-moon, seemed to peer down at the driveway like a single, unblinking eye.

Gingerbread trim, once whimsical and inviting, now hung from the eaves in tragic disrepair. Ivy had begun its slow conquest of the eastern wall, its tendrils probing between boards and around window frames as if the forest itself was trying to reclaim the structure.

A chimney rose from the center of the roof, listing slightly to one side. Even vacant and empty, it seemed to exhale a faint wisp of smoke, a ghostly breath that dissipated into the heavy air surrounding the property.

Dark clouds loomed over the solemn structure nestled in Willow Creek's shadowed heart. Tom's hands, calloused and firm, delved into the vehicle's depths, drawing out cardboard boxes marked with memories and necessity. Beside him, Lisa's eyes, shadowed by strands of dark hair, carried a glimmer of hope as she grabbed a box and surveyed their fresh start.

Emily and Jake tumbled out of the backseat, their laughter slicing through the thick forest air. Emily grabbed Jake's hand, pulling him along as she raced to explore every corner of the wrap-around porch.

Emily darted ahead, her sneakers crunching on the gravel. She skidded to a stop before a grimy window, her breath fogging the glass.

"Whoa," she whispered, green eyes wide. "It's like the house is wearing sunglasses."

Her small hands pressed against the pane, leaving ghostly prints in years of dust. As she leaned in, her nose touched the cool surface, and she giggled at the gritty texture.

"Mom! Dad!" Emily called over her shoulder, excitement bubbling in her voice. "I think the inside's even spookier than the outside!"

Jake hung back by the porch steps, his gaze drawn to the wall of trees hemming in their new home. Twisted branches stretched overhead like a net of dark fingers, and somewhere in that leafy gloom, crows muttered harsh secrets to each other. Jake's shoulders tensed, and he edged closer to his sister. "Em," he whispered, tugging at her sleeve. "I don't like it here. The trees look...mean."

Emily turned, her exploration of the grimy windows forgotten as she saw the worry etched on her little brother's face. She grabbed his hand, giving it a squeeze. "Aw, come on, Jake. They're just trees," she said, but her voice held a note of uncertainty as her eyes flicked to the looming forest. She puffed out her chest, faking a confidence she didn't quite feel. "Tell you what — bet I can beat you to that big oak over there!"

Without waiting for a response, Emily took off running, pulling a reluctant Jake along behind her. She skidded to a stop beneath the massive oak, Jake panting as he caught up. They tilted their heads back, taking in the sprawling canopy overhead. Twisted branches creaked in the breeze, a sound like old bones stretching.

"See?" Emily said, her voice a little too bright. "Just a big ol' tree."

But even as the words left her mouth, Emily felt a prickle of gooseflesh rais the hair on her arms. The leaves seemed to whisper secrets to each other, and the shadows... were they always this dark, this alive?

Jake pressed closer to his sister, his eyes darting from tree to tree. "Can we go back now?" he mumbled.

Emily nodded, trying to swallow the lump in her throat. "Yeah," she said softly. "Let's go see if Mom needs help unpacking."

As they turned to leave, neither child saw the pair of gleaming eyes watching them from a hollow in the oak's trunk.

They hurried back towards the house, leaves crunching under their feet. A breeze picked up, cool fingers of air playing with their hair and clothes. Emily thought she heard something in that wind — a whisper, maybe? Or was it...

Jake suddenly gripped her hand tighter. "Did you hear that?" he asked, his voice barely audible.

Emily wanted to say no, to tell him it was just the wind in the trees. But she couldn't shake the feeling that the sound they'd heard was laughter — faint, wild, and not quite human.

"Come on," she said instead, picking up her pace. "I'll race you back to the porch!"

They ran, the wind chasing them all the way to the house, carrying secrets neither of them was ready to hear.

———————

The next morning, Tom woke before dawn as he did every weekday. He dressed quietly in the dark, careful not to disturb Lisa. As he knotted his tie and ran a comb through his hair, he stared at his reflection in the bathroom mirror. The face staring back at him looked tired. The spark of youth had long faded from his eyes. With a quiet sigh, he turned and made his way downstairs.

In the kitchen, he prepared a simple breakfast — black coffee and two pieces of toast. He ate quickly, and mechanically, his mind already running through the tedious tasks that awaited him at work. Emails to answer, reports to file, meetings to sit through. The same routine day after day, each blending into the next until he could barely distinguish one from the other.

After rinsing his plate and mug in the sink, Tom grabbed his jacket and keys. He paused in the entryway, gazing up the stairs. For a moment, he considered going back, slipping under the covers to wrap his arms around Lisa, breathing in the scent of her hair. But no — she needed her rest, and he had to go.

Stepping outside, Tom shivered against the pre-dawn chill. His breath misted in the crisp morning air as he walked to the driveway. The road was empty, the neighborhood silent except for the calls of early birds. He started his car and pulled away, the rumble of the engine shattering the stillness. As the house disappeared from view, an unease settled over him that had nothing to do with the long day ahead.

Somewhere in the woods, something watched him go.

An hour later, in the studio, Lisa sat surrounded by her paintings. Dozens of canvases leaned against the walls, bursts of vibrant color shining in the morning light. She picked up a brush, contemplating the half-finished landscape on the easel before her. A forest scene, the trees were rendered in moody greens and deep blues. It was meant to capture the mysterious allure of the woods behind their new home, but the shadows she'd painted now seemed almost sinister.

With a frustrated sigh, Lisa set her brush down again. No matter how vividly she saw each image in her mind's eye, it never quite translated onto the canvas. Her dreams of being a professional artist, of having her work displayed in galleries, seemed to slip further away with each failed painting. She glanced at the stack of bills on her desk, the envelopes glowing accusatorily white. Some were stamped "Final Notice" in red. The money Tom brought in each month was barely enough for their family of four. If only her art could sell...

Downstairs, Emily and Jake huddled by the front door, backpacks slumped at their feet. Jake couldn't stop fidgeting, his fingers twisting the hem of his t-shirt. Emily, on the other hand, was a whirlwind of excitement.

"Jake, you're gonna love it!" She bounced on her toes. "I heard they've got this ginormous playground. Monkey bars, swings, the works! And get this—there's an art room. Easels, paints, even clay!"

Her voice filled the quiet hallway, a stream of chatter meant to wash away her little brother's worries. But Jake's eyes kept drifting to the window, watching the trees sway in the morning breeze.

"Em?" His voice was barely a whisper. "What if...what if the bus gets lost? All these woods look the same."

Emily wrapped an arm around Jake's shoulders, giving him a quick squeeze. "No way, little bro. Buses have special forest-proof GPS or something. They never get lost."

Jake nodded but didn't look convinced.

As they stepped outside to wait, Emily's eyes swept over the sea of pines surrounding their new home. For a moment, the trees seemed to press closer, their branches reaching, grasping. She shook her head, pushing the thought away.

But as the yellow bus finally rumbled into view, a small voice in the back of Emily's mind whispered, "What if Jake's right?"

———

It had been a long day at school. The school bus wheezed to a stop at the corner of Maple and Oak, and Emily practically dragged Jake off, her backpack bouncing wildly. "Come on, slowpoke! Let's explore!"

Jake stumbled after her, eyes wide. "But Em, shouldn't we go home?"

Emily waved off his concern. "Mom said we could look around as long as we're back for dinner. Now, come on!"

They ambled down Main Street, Emily's head swiveling like an owl's. The quaint storefronts looked like something out of an old movie. "Ooh, look!" Emily pointed at a dusty antique shop. "I bet that place is full of magical artifacts. Maybe even a genie lamp!"

Jake peered through the grimy window. "I don't see any lamps, but there's a creepy old doll that I think just blinked at me."

Emily giggled. "You and your imagination!"

They continued on, passing a small park where a group of kids were playing. "Hey, Em," Jake tugged her sleeve. "D'you think they go to our school?"

Emily shrugged. "Maybe. We can ask them tomorrow if we see them."

As they rounded the corner to the town square, Emily gasped. In the center stood a massive oak tree, its branches stretching out like a giant umbrella.

"Whoa," Jake whispered. "It's huge!"

Emily nodded, her eyes gleaming. "I bet it's magic. Like, maybe it grants wishes if you whisper to it at midnight."

Jake frowned. "I dunno, Em. Remember what happened last time you made a wish?"

Emily's face fell for a moment, but she quickly brightened. "This is different. C'mon, let's get a closer look!"

As they approached the tree, an old woman on a nearby bench smiled at them. "New in town, are you?"

Emily beamed. "Yes, ma'am! I'm Emily and this is my brother Jake. We just moved into the old house on Willow Lane."

The woman's smile faltered for a split second. "Oh, I see. Well, welcome to Willow Creek. I'm Mrs. Abernathy."

Jake, who had been quiet, suddenly spoke up. "Mrs. Abernathy, why does everyone look scared when we mention our house?"

Emily elbowed him, but Mrs. Abernathy just chuckled. "Oh, don't mind us old folks. We just love our ghost stories. Now, you two best be getting home before dark. The shadows get a bit tricky around here after sunset."

As they walked away, Emily's mind raced with possibilities. "Jake! What if our house is haunted? How cool would that be?"

Jake shuddered. "Not cool, Em. Not cool at all."

The sun was playing hide-and-seek behind the trees as Emily and Jake made their way home. Emily zigzagged along the path, her pockets clinking with "treasure" — interesting rocks and acorns she'd collected. Jake trudged behind, his eyes darting from shadow to shadow.

As they approached the old Victorian, the smell of roast chicken and fresh bread drifted through the open windows. Inside, they found their mom in the kitchen, flour dusting her apron like snow, while their dad was hunched over a stack of papers at the table, his forehead creased.

"There are my explorers!" Lisa's smile was warm but tired. "Go on, wash up. Dinner's almost ready."

Soon, the family gathered around the old wooden table, its surface a map of scratches and stains. Lisa broke the silence. "So, how was everyone's day? The market was... interesting. Lots of curious folks, even if they weren't buying yet."

Tom nodded, swallowing a mouthful. "Quiet town. Seems...nice enough." He paused, then added with forced cheer, "Good place for a fresh start, right?"

Emily bounced in her seat, words tumbling out like marbles. "Oh! And we met this super nice old lady today! Mrs. Abernathy. She told us Willow Creek's full of ghost stories and haunted places and—"

"Whoa there, speed racer," Tom cut in with a chuckle. "Let's not go chasing shadows, alright?"

Emily's eyes sparkled. "But Dad, what if the ghosts need our help? Like in my stories!"

Jake hunched lower, pushing peas around his plate like a miniature bulldozer.

Lisa reached over, her hand warm on Jake's. "Hey, sweetie. You've been awful quiet. Everything okay?"

Jake shrugged, not meeting her eyes. "I guess. It's just... the woods feel weird here. Kinda scary."

"Oh, honey," Lisa's voice softened. "Big changes are always a bit unsettling. You'll get used to it, I promise."

Tom cleared his throat, straightening in his chair. "Look, ghost stories aside, this move is going to be good for us. A fresh start, remember?"

A chorus of half-hearted "yeahs" echoed around the table. Despite the undercurrent of worry, there was a warmth in the air, a fragile hope. The family lingered, savoring the comfort of being together.

CHAPTER 2
MALATHOR'S WELL

Emily and Jake ventured into the dense forest surrounding their new home, drawn by the mysterious allure of the woods. Emily led the way, her feet light on the narrow dirt path, her bright eyes darting from tree to tree as she imagined the wonders and secrets hidden within the forest's depths. Jake followed close behind, caught between excitement for adventure and a growing sense of unease.

As they pressed deeper into the woods, the ancient canopy above grew thicker, filtering out more and more sunlight. Strange sounds echoed around them—the snap of breaking branches, the rustle of unseen creatures, and occasional eerie cries that neither child could identify. Here and there, shafts of light pierced the gloom like spotlights, illuminating swirling dust motes and gossamer strands of spider silk stretched between gnarled trunks.

Emily stopped to look around at the spooky forest. "Wow, Jake! Look at this place!" she said in a loud whisper. "It's just like in my storybooks. There could be fairies hiding anywhere!"

Jake nodded but found himself inching closer to his sister. There was something watchful about these woods that set his nerves on edge. He wished they had thought to mark their path, suddenly aware of how easy it would be to lose their way.

Just as Jake was about to say they should go back, Emily's face lit up. "Oh! Look over there!" she shouted, suddenly running ahead.

She charged forward, heedless of the thorns and branches that scratched at her bare legs. Between two ancient oaks, a crumbling stone structure came into view. Jake hurried to keep up, his sense of foreboding growing with each step.

"Emily, hold on!" he yelled, but his sister was already racing toward the strange thing they'd found, too curious to stop.

They burst into a small clearing, where rays of sunlight pierced through the leafy canopy above. In the center stood an ancient stone well, its weathered surface draped in vines that coiled around the rim like bony fingers.

"Whoa, check it out!" Emily gasped, scampering around the well with eyes as wide as saucers. Her small hands explored the mossy stones while Jake hung back, eyeing his sister nervously. Something about this place made his stomach do flip-flops, though he couldn't quite figure out why.

Emily stood on her tiptoes, trying to peer into the well's depths, but saw only inky blackness. As she circled the structure, she spotted a wooden sign nailed above it. Squinting at the faded letters, she read aloud: "Be Careful What You Wish For."

"Jake! Come here!" Emily called excitedly. "It's like something out of a fairy tale—a real wishing well!"

Jake inched closer, frowning at the sign. "I dunno, Em," he said, his voice wobbling slightly. "This place gives me the creeps. Maybe we should go."

But Emily was lost in her own world of imagination, already dreaming up wishes. She squeezed her eyes shut and fished a coin from her pocket, her thumb tracing its ridged edge as she held it like a talisman of infinite possibility.

Emily stared at the well, her mind whirling with possibilities. She thought about how Dad always looked tired after work and how Mom's beautiful paintings just sat in the art studio. She remembered overhearing her parents whispering worriedly about bills late at night.

A tiny spark of hope flickered in her chest. Maybe she could fix everything!

"Jake," she said, her voice barely above a whisper, "what if we could make everything better? For Mom and Dad, for all of us?"

Jake frowned, shuffling his feet. "I don't know, Em. Remember that story Grandma told us? About the monkey's paw? Wishes always go wrong in stories."

But Emily wasn't really listening. Her eyes were fixed on the dark depths of the well, imagining all the good things that could happen.

"It'll be different this time," she insisted. "I'll be super careful with my words. I can make everything okay again!"

Jake reached for her arm. "Emily, wait—"

But Emily's mind was made up. She bit her lip, trying to think of the perfect wish that would solve all their problems.

The shiny quarter caught the sunlight in Emily's palm, casting tiny sparkles across her face. She held it up, letting the sunlight glint off its surface. Her eyes squeezed shut, face scrunched in concentration.

Taking a deep breath, she spoke in a clear voice that rang with hope: "I wish... I wish for my whole family to be happy forever and ever!"

Jake watched, his face a mix of worry and curiosity. "Em, are you sure about this?"

But Emily had already made up her mind. With a flick of her wrist, she tossed the coin into the well.

For a heartbeat, everything went quiet. The forest seemed to hold its breath. Then came a small 'plink' as the coin hit the water far below.

The sound echoed up the stone walls, growing stranger and louder instead of fading away. It bounced around them, making the air feel thick and heavy.

Emily's eyes flew open, darting between the well and her brother. "Did you hear that?" she whispered.

Jake nodded slowly, his eyes wide. "Yeah...that was weird."

As the strange echo faded away, something in the air seemed to change. A cool breeze whispered through the trees, rustling leaves and carrying faint, unrecognizable sounds. Emily shivered, goosebumps prickling along her arms. She felt excited but also a little scared, like the moment before opening a big present.

Jake tugged at her sleeve. "Come on, Em," he said, his voice shaky. "We should go home now."

Emily nodded but couldn't resist one last peek at the well. As she turned, a flicker of movement caught her eye. For just a second, she thought she saw something dark shifting deep inside the well. She blinked hard, shaking her head.

"Just my imagination," she muttered to herself.

"What?" Jake asked, already backing away.

"Nothing," Emily said quickly. "Let's go."

They hurried out of the clearing, twigs snapping under their feet. Emily's mind raced with all the wonderful things that might happen now. Her wish had to come true, right?

But Jake kept glancing over his shoulder, unable to shake the feeling that something wasn't quite right. As they rushed home, the shadows between the trees seemed to grow darker, reaching out with long fingers as if trying to grab them.

CHAPTER 3
MALATHOR'S WELL

Golden morning light streamed through the kitchen windows, casting a warm glow over the Porter family's breakfast table. The air hummed with an unusual energy, a stark contrast to the tense mornings they'd grown accustomed to since moving to Willow Creek.

Tom's phone buzzed against the worn wooden tabletop. As he answered, his face transformed, worry lines smoothing out into a broad smile. Simultaneously, Lisa's phone chimed with an email that made her drop her toast, her hand flying to her mouth in shock.

"I got the promotion!" Tom announced, his voice cracking with excitement.

Lisa's eyes sparkled with joyful disbelief. "And someone just bought three of my paintings. For more than I ever dreamed!"

Emily watched her parents from behind her cereal bowl, barely containing a knowing smirk. The wish she'd made at the old well had worked its magic. The heavy cloud that had been hanging over their family was finally lifting.

Tom set down his phone, running a hand through his disheveled hair. "Well, would you look at that? Our luck is finally turning around!"

Lisa nodded, absently stirring her cooling coffee. "After all this time... I'd almost given up hope."

Emily shoveled another heaping spoonful of soggy cereal into her mouth. "See? Willow Creek isn't so bad after all," she mumbled, milk dribbling down her chin.

Tom chuckled, reaching over to ruffle her tangled bedhead. "Hey, no talking with your mouth full, squirt. But you're right. This might be exactly the fresh start we needed."

The cheerful atmosphere persisted throughout the morning. Tom whistled an upbeat tune while knotting his tie, and Lisa hummed softly as she wiped down the kitchen counters. After waving goodbye to her parents from the porch, Emily tugged on her bright yellow rain boots, excitement bubbling in her chest at the thought of exploring more of the mysterious woods surrounding their new home.

As she bounded down the creaky porch steps, she failed to notice Jake watching her from their bedroom window, a worried frown creasing his young face.

Emily spent the rest of the day exploring the woods, her heart filled with a newfound sense of hope. As she returned home in the late afternoon, she noticed Jake's worried gaze from the window and gave him a reassuring smile.

———

A week later, Lisa stood in her studio, carefully wrapping her prized paintings in crinkly brown paper. Her fingers, stained with smudges of vibrant oils, worked deftly as she secured each piece.

"I can't believe this is really happening," Lisa murmured to herself, a smile playing on her lips. She paused, holding up a haunting landscape of Willow Creek's misty forests. The gallery owner's words echoed in her mind: "Your work captures something...otherworldly. It's perfect for our autumn showcase."

Across town, Tom straightened his silk tie, its deep blue a stark contrast against his crisp white shirt. He took a deep breath, squaring his shoulders before pushing open the heavy oak door of the executive conference room. The hum of conversation died down as he entered.

"Good morning, everyone," Tom said, his voice steady despite the flutter in his stomach. "Let's dive into this week's numbers, shall we?"

As he spoke, pointing out key metrics on the projected slides, he noticed approving nods from the CEO. A warm glow of pride spread through his chest. Under his guidance, the company was thriving.

Back at home, the sound of children's laughter filled the air. Emily and Jake sprawled on the plush new area rug, surrounded by a small sea of toys still gleaming with that fresh-from-the-box shine.

"Watch this, Em!" Jake exclaimed, fingers flying over the controls of his new robot. The toy whirred to life, executing a perfect backflip.

Emily clapped, her eyes shining. "That's so cool! I bet I can make mine do a handstand!"

As they played, Emily couldn't help but feel a swell of satisfaction. This was all because of her wish, she thought. Their lives had changed so much, and it was all thanks to her.

As twilight descended on Willow Creek, shadows lengthened across the Porter home. In her studio, Lisa hunched over her easel, her brow furrowed in concentration. The scratch of bristles against canvas filled the air, accompanied by the soft clink of brushes in a water jar.

Suddenly, a clatter shattered Lisa's concentration. Her brushes, meticulously arranged just moments ago, now lay strewn across the floor. "What on earth?" she murmured, bending to gather them. As she straightened, an unsettling prickle crawled across her skin as if invisible fingers were tracing her outline. Lisa spun around, her heart thundering in her chest, only to be confronted by the familiar sight of blank canvases propped against the wall. In the waning daylight, their pristine white surfaces seemed to glow with an ethereal luminescence.

Shaking her head, Lisa returned to her painting. But something felt off. Her usually graceful strokes felt clumsy, the vibrant colors she'd mixed earlier now appearing dull and lifeless on the canvas. Frustration mounted with each unsuccessful attempt to capture her vision.

"I just need some air," she sighed, setting down her palette with a soft thud.

As Lisa stepped outside, the wind whipped her hair into a frenzy. Ominous clouds roiled overhead, obscuring the stars. She hugged herself tightly, shivering in the sudden chill. Moonlight filtered through the clouds, casting an otherworldly glow on the twisted branches of nearby trees. They seemed to reach for her with gnarled fingers, creaking in the wind. A low, mournful hoot echoed from the woods, sending another shiver through her.

The shadows around her studio wavered as if alive. Lisa blinked hard, telling herself it was just a trick of the light. But as she turned to retreat inside, her blood ran cold. The doorknob refused to turn, unyielding beneath her increasingly frantic twists.

"No, no, no," she whispered, rattling the handle violently. From within came the sound of shattering glass. The metal grew icy against her palm, burning with cold.

"Tom!" Lisa cried out, fear tightening her throat. "The door—it's stuck!" She pounded her fists against the unyielding wood until they throbbed with pain. Just as panic threatened to overwhelm her, the knob suddenly gave way. The door swung open with a prolonged creak, revealing her studio, dimly lit and utterly still.

Gasping for air, Lisa stumbled inside. She sagged

against the wall, her heart racing. As her breathing slowly steadied, she couldn't shake the creeping sensation that something was terribly, inexplicably wrong.

In the shadows of the room, unnoticed by Lisa, a dark shape seemed to writhe for a moment before melting back into stillness.

Meanwhile, in his home office, Tom hunched over a sprawling array of reports, his pen scratching rhythmically against paper—the sole intrusion on the twilight hush. Without warning, the fine hairs on his nape prickled to attention, a silent alarm triggering in his subconscious. A ghostly current of air whispered through the room, sending the carefully arranged documents on his desk into a frenzied dance, their edges fluttering like agitated butterfly wings.

Struggling to rationalize the inexplicable, Tom vigorously rubbed his arms, desperate to generate warmth in the suddenly frigid room. "Why is it so damn cold in here?" he muttered, his words materializing as wispy clouds before him. The air had taken on an oppressive quality, heavy with moisture that seemed to seep into his bones. It reminded him of the dank chill of a subterranean cavern. Brow furrowed, Tom pushed himself up from his chair, wincing at its plaintive creak, and strode to the thermostat. The digital display glowed an obstinate 72 degrees, mocking his discomfort and defying the room's arctic transformation.

A soft thud behind him made Tom spin around, his heart leaping into his throat. A heavy, leather-bound book lay on the floor, its ornate cover glinting in the lamplight. Tom's brow furrowed as he bent to pick it up. The cover depicted an ancient stone well, surrounded by indistinct, shadowy figures that seemed to writhe under his gaze.

"That's odd," Tom said, his voice unnaturally loud in the stillness. "I don't remember this book."

As he opened it, his stomach lurched. The pages were filled with arcane symbols and disturbing illustrations that made his head swim. Hastily, he shoved the book back onto the shelf, his hands trembling slightly.

No sooner had he turned away than a sound made him freeze. A faint whisper, barely audible, seemed to emanate from the walls themselves. Tom shook his head vigorously. "It's just the house settling," he told himself, but the words rang hollow in the oppressive silence.

Returning to his desk, Tom tried to focus on his work, but the whispers persisted. They grew in volume, surrounding him, unintelligible yet somehow threatening. Goosebumps erupted across his skin as the temperature plummeted further. The shadows in the corners of the room seemed to deepen and shift as if concealing watchful presences.

Tom's breath came in short, sharp gasps as the whispers drew closer, circling him like predators stalking their prey. The lamp flickered, plunging the room into momentary darkness. When the light returned, Tom could have sworn he saw a dark figure standing in the corner, gone in an instant.

"Hello?" he called out, his voice cracking. "Is someone there?"

Tom's question hung in the air, met only by the persistent, maddening whispers that seemed to mock his growing fear.

These ethereal murmurs swelled, their intensity building like a rising tide. They ricocheted off the walls, filling the room with a cacophony of unintelligible voices as if the very house had awakened and found its own unsettling language. Tom's heart raced, each thunderous beat threatening to burst from his chest, a primal drum echoing in counterpoint to the supernatural chorus. His eyes, wide with a mixture of disbelief and terror, darted frantically around the room. They searched desperately for some tangible source of the unnatural sounds but found only the once-comforting familiarity of shadow-draped corners and empty spaces, now sinister in their apparent innocence.

A bone-deep chill slithered down his spine, raising goosebumps on his skin. The temperature plummeted, turning his ragged breaths into ghostly plumes of white vapor. An unsettling sensation crept over him—invisible eyes scrutinizing his every twitch and tremor.

The shadows in the corners began to writhe and twist, morphing into grotesque, claw-like forms that seemed to reach out towards him. Tom stood frozen, his gaze locked on the deepening darkness. From within the inky void, a tall, gaunt figure began to take shape. Tom squeezed his eyes shut, praying it was merely a trick of his overtaxed mind. But when he looked again, the emaciated creature remained, its hollow eyes boring into the very depths of his soul.

"Lisa?" Tom called out, his voice barely above a whisper. "Are you there?"

The silence that answered him was more terrifying than any sound could have been.

Tom stumbled backward, colliding with his desk and sending his chair clattering to the floor. The entity drifted forward, its elongated arms unfurling like ribbons of shadow. A wave of nauseating breath engulfed Tom, and he retched at the foul stench. His mind reeled, desperately clinging to reason.

"This isn't real," he muttered, voice trembling. "It can't be."

Squeezing his eyes shut, Tom concentrated on banishing the apparition. When he finally summoned the courage to look again, the room was empty. The whispers had vanished, leaving behind a deafening silence broken only by his ragged breathing. His pulse still raced as he surveyed the undisturbed room, grappling with what he'd witnessed.

"Was it real?" he wondered aloud, his words hanging in the air. "Or am I losing my mind?"

The uncertainty of which answer was more terrifying gnawed at him, leaving Tom feeling more alone and vulnerable than ever before.

———

Days later, an air of unease settled over Lisa as she attempted to prepare dinner. The raw chicken lay forgotten on the counter while her gaze was drawn to the window. Despite the early hour, an unnatural darkness had descended upon the yard. Wind whipped through the skeleton-like branches of the old oak tree, its limbs stretching toward the house like gnarled, grasping fingers.

A sudden crash from the living room startled Lisa from her reverie. She rushed in to find Emily standing by the fireplace, her eyes wide with shock. Shards of glass from a shattered photo frame lay scattered on the floor.

"Mom, I didn't touch it, I promise!" Emily blurted out, her voice quivering. "It just...flew off the mantle by itself."

Lisa's response died in her throat as a shadow swept through the room, accompanied by an icy draft. The walls seemed to come alive with whispers, growing louder and more insistent with each passing moment. Jake, sensing the tension, let out a soft whimper and pressed himself against Lisa's side.

"What's going on?" Emily asked, her earlier bravado crumbling in the face of the inexplicable.

Lisa shook her head, at a loss for words. She longed to reassure her children, to convince them — and herself — that everything was fine. But the encroaching shadows and bizarre occurrences told a different story. A malevolent presence had taken root in their new home, and Lisa feared they were powerless against its growing influence.

"I... I'm not sure, sweetheart," Lisa finally managed, her voice barely above a whisper. She pulled both children close, as much for her own comfort as theirs. "But we'll figure it out together, okay?" Lisa couldn't shake the feeling that this was only the beginning of their ordeal.

The shadows retreated as swiftly as they had appeared, leaving the family huddled together in a state of bewildered fear. Emily's eyes darted around the room, wide with apprehension. "It felt...wrong, Mom. Like something bad is here."

Jake nodded solemnly, still clinging to his mother. Lisa gently stroked his hair, wishing she could brush away his fears as easily as she smoothed his tousled locks.

Tom stood watching from the doorway, his brow furrowed in concern. He cleared his throat, his practical nature visibly at odds with the inexplicable events they'd just witnessed. "I'm sure there's a logical explanation," he offered, his voice wavering slightly despite his attempt at reassurance. "Old houses often make strange noises. That's probably all it was."

Lisa's eyes met Tom's, and she saw the same uncertainty reflected there. Tom's pragmatism made him reluctant to entertain supernatural explanations, but Lisa had seen the shadows move with deliberate, menacing purpose. She had felt the malevolence behind the bone-chilling cold that had enveloped them.

As they finally managed to calm the children enough for bed, Lisa couldn't shake a growing sense of dread. She tucked Emily and Jake in, making a show of checking for monsters under the bed and in the closet. Their room appeared normal now — toys strewn across the floor, soft moonlight filtering through the curtains. But Lisa knew that whatever had invaded their home was still present, biding its time before the next terrifying manifestation.

"Goodnight, sweethearts," Lisa said, forcing a smile. "Try to get some sleep, okay?"

She resisted the urge to stand guard over them, instead stepping out into the hallway where she nearly collided with Tom. He emerged from their bedroom, his face ashen.

"The temperature just plummeted in there," he murmured, his eyes wide. "And I could've sworn the walls were...pulsating. Lisa, we need to figure this out before it escalates."

Lisa nodded grimly. "Tomorrow," she agreed. "We'll start looking for answers first thing in the morning."

As they retreated to their room, Lisa felt a chill that had nothing to do with the temperature. She was now certain that something sinister had followed them to Willow Creek. If they didn't act quickly, she feared, none of them would ever feel safe in their own home again.

CHAPTER 4
MALATHOR'S WELL

Jake's fork traced aimless patterns through his green beans, his supper untouched. Shadows lurked beneath his eyes, a testament to another night spent wrestling with unseen terrors. Emily watched her brother, concern etching lines on her young face. Jake had always been a solitary child, but lately, he seemed to inhabit a world entirely his own.

"You should eat, Jakey," Emily coaxed, her voice gentle. "You'll need your strength today."

Jake remained unresponsive, his gaze fixed on some distant point beyond the faded wallpaper. Emily followed his stare but saw only peeling flowers and the ghosts of past decades.

The stairs groaned, heralding their father's arrival. Tom paused in the doorway, absorbing the scene before him. His eyes met Lisa's, and a current of unspoken worry passed between them. Their son was fading, becoming a stranger before their very eyes.

"Evening, kids," Tom said, his smile not quite reaching his eyes. Jake remained motionless, but Emily's face brightened.

"Evening, Daddy! I made supper all by myself!"

Tom's hand found Emily's hair, tousling it affectionately as he took his seat. Silence descended, broken only by the mournful clink of cutlery against china.

Without warning, Jake's shriek shattered the quiet. His chair clattered to the floor as he scrambled backward, pressing himself against the wall. His wild eyes fixed on an empty corner, seeing horrors invisible to the rest of them.

"Jake!" Lisa cried, rushing to him. "What's wrong, sweetheart?"

But Jake seemed oblivious to her presence, his gaze locked on his private nightmare.

"Go away!" he screamed, his voice raw with terror. "Leave me alone!"

Emily hovered nearby, her hands twisting anxiously. "It's okay, Jakey," she soothed. "You're safe. Nothing can hurt you."

Jake's frightened eyes snapped to his sister, accusation blazing in their depths. "This is all your fault!" he spat. "You let it out! Now it's coming for me!"

Emily recoiled as if struck, her face crumpling. "No, I didn't mean to..."

But Jake had retreated once more, soft whimpers escaping as he stared into the seemingly empty corner. Tom's hand found Emily's shoulder, offering silent comfort as they watched Lisa's futile attempts to soothe their tormented son.

Lisa sank to the floor beside Jake, enveloping his quivering form in a protective embrace. His eyes, wide and glassy with terror, remained fixed on the seemingly empty corner.

"There's nothing there, sweetie," Lisa murmured, her voice a soothing whisper. "Whatever you're seeing, it can't hurt you."

Jake's head whipped from side to side in frantic denial. "It's there," he insisted, his voice trembling. "I can feel it watching me. It's so angry." His small fingers twisted into Lisa's shirt, clinging desperately.

Overhead, the ceiling light flickered ominously. Emily's gaze darted upward, apprehension etching her features as grotesque shadows cavorted across the walls. The lightbulb emitted an angry buzz before surrendering to darkness, plunging the kitchen into an inky void.

Jake's whimper pierced the sudden gloom as he burrowed closer to his mother. Tom lurched to his feet, fumbling for the flashlight they now kept by the back door. But before his fingers could close around it, the bulb detonated in a vicious spray of glass.

Lisa's scream pierced the air as she curled her body around Jake, shielding him from the glittering shrapnel raining down. Emily pressed herself against the wall, her heart a frenzied drum in her chest.

"What's happening?" she cried, her voice raw with fear.

A low, menacing creak emanated from above. Emily's terrified gaze tracked upward to find the overhead light swinging in a violent arc. The cords groaned under the strain, then snapped with a sound like a gunshot. The entire fixture plummeted, crashing to the floor mere inches from Tom's feet.

The Porter family huddled together on the kitchen floor, shock rendering them mute. As dust motes settled in the aftermath, the cacophony of rattling and shaking subsided. An unnatural silence descended, punctuated only by their ragged, panicked breaths. They exchanged glances, dawning comprehension reflected in their wide eyes. This was no mere electrical malfunction or structural flaw. Something malevolent had invaded their home, turning their sanctuary into a battleground of unseen forces.

An oppressive silence descended upon the house, heavy and expectant, like the world holding its breath before a tempest breaks. Emily, drawn by an irresistible mixture of fear and fascination, inched towards the glittering debris of the shattered light fixture. Her hands quivered, but her eyes gleamed with a dangerous curiosity. What malevolent force could have wreaked such havoc? She extended a trembling finger towards a wickedly sharp shard of glass, hesitating on the precipice of contact.

"Don't touch it!" Tom's voice cracked like a whip, sharp with urgency. In one fluid motion, he swept Emily behind the barricade of his body, shepherding her back towards Lisa and Jake. His broad shoulders were coiled with tension, jaw clenched in a rictus of barely contained terror.

A gelid draft slithered through the room, its icy fingers tousling their hair with malicious playfulness. Gooseflesh erupted across Emily's arms, a primal response to an unseen threat. Peering around her father's protective stance, her gaze was drawn inexorably to the back door. It swung lazily on its hinges, each creaking oscillation a taunt. Emily's heart lurched painfully in her chest as a chilling realization dawned. That door had been locked, hadn't it? Her eyes, wide with dawning horror, sought out her mother's equally terrified gaze. Neither of them had unlocked that door. Which could only mean one thing...

Something had let itself in.

A glacial current of air washed over Emily, eliciting an involuntary shudder. Her fingers twisted into the fabric of her father's shirt as she peered around his protective bulk towards the yawning maw of the open door. Beyond the threshold lay an impenetrable wall of darkness, as if the night itself had coalesced into a tangible entity.

Tom shifted his weight, his body a living shield as he reached for another flashlight. His fingers closed around the cold metal, and he flicked the switch with a desperate hope. Nothing. The darkness remained unbroken. A muffled curse escaped his lips as he struck the device against his palm, willing it to life. But no comforting beam emerged to pierce the oppressive gloom.

A soft scuttling whispered from the doorway to the living room, barely perceptible over the thunderous beating of their hearts. Something was stirring in that inky void, its movements sending chills down their spines. Jake's whimper cut through the silence, his small hands burrowing into Lisa's arms with frightened intensity. She drew him closer, her fingers combing through his hair in a futile attempt at comfort.

"Tom..." Lisa's voice was a taut wire of fear, ready to snap at any moment.

He rose slowly, arm outstretched to ward his family back. "Stay behind me," he commanded, his voice low and strained.

Drawing a shaky breath, Tom inched towards the interior door. Emily's grip on her mother's hand tightened to the point of pain as she craned her neck, desperate for a glimpse past her father's silhouette. The waiting was unbearable, each second stretching into an eternity of dreadful anticipation.

Tom hesitated at the threshold, leaning forward to peer into the murk. "There's nothing—" His words morphed into a strangled cry as an unseen force violently wrenched him into the darkness.

"Tom!" Lisa's scream tore through the air.

Emily lunged forward instinctively, but her mother's iron grip held her back. Jake's wails reached a fever pitch, his hysteria a perfect counterpoint to the vicious sounds of struggle from outside. Their father's cries of pain mingled with the sickening thuds and crashes of combat against an unseen foe.

Then, as suddenly as it began, it stopped. An unnatural silence descended, more terrifying than any noise could have been.

Lisa's breath snagged in her throat, a war raging within

her. The primal need to find Tom warred against her instinct to protect her children. Jake's inconsolable wails continued to pierce the air, his small frame wracked with tremors.

"Emily," Lisa's voice was taut with urgency, "stay with your brother. Lock the door behind me, and don't open it for anyone but me or your father." She fumbled in the drawer, fingers closing around the cold metal of another flashlight. Emily's eyes were wide pools of fear, but she nodded with a bravery that belied her years.

Steeling herself against the unknown, Lisa ventured into the oppressive darkness of the house. Her heart thundered in her chest, its frantic rhythm echoing in her ears as she swept the flashlight beam across the silent rooms. The shadows seemed to writhe and retreat from the light, but there was no sign of Tom or his mysterious assailant.

With painstaking caution, she inched her way through the living room and into the parlor. A low groan emanated from the corner, causing her to start violently. The flashlight beam sliced through the gloom, revealing Tom's crumpled form on the floor. One hand was pressed against a rapidly swelling lump on the back of his head.

"Tom!" Lisa's cry was a mixture of relief and renewed fear as she rushed to his side, helping him into a sitting position. "What happened?"

Tom winced, his fingers gingerly probing the tender welt. "Something...something struck me from behind," he muttered, his voice thick with pain. "I must have blacked out. I think it's gone now, whatever it was."

Lisa gently eased him to his feet, her mind racing. "We need to get you to a hospital. The children—"

Her words were cut short by a thunderous crash from upstairs. The kitchen door flew open with a bang, and Emily and Jake burst into the room, their faces masks of terror as they huddled against their parents. The family clung to each other, a small island of humanity in a sea of encroaching darkness.

Lisa and Tom exchanged a look of abject terror as another thunderous crash reverberated from upstairs, the sound seeming to shake the very foundations of the house.

"We need to get out of here. Now." Tom's voice was steel-wrapped in pain as he struggled to his feet, his face contorting with the effort.

Lisa braced him as they hurried towards the front door. The children huddled close behind like frightened ducklings. Emily's heart pounded a frantic rhythm in her ears, drowning out all else. What unholy force was wreaking such havoc upstairs? She craned her neck as they passed the staircase, desperate for a glimpse of the upper landing, but it remained cloaked in impenetrable shadow.

They burst into the frigid night air, their breaths forming ghostly plumes in the darkness. Tom sagged against the car, his labored breathing punctuated by soft groans. A thin rivulet of blood snaked down from the angry welt on his head, glistening black in the moonlight.

"Oh, Tom," Lisa's voice quavered with worry as she fumbled in her purse, her trembling hands searching for the elusive keys.

A blood-curdling screech tore through the night, freezing them in place. Lisa's hand stilled, the keys dangling uselessly from her fingers. Emily felt her insides crystallize with dread. As one, they slowly raised their eyes to the looming silhouette of the house.

An ethereal face peered out from an upstairs window, its features blurred and indistinct, more smoke than substance. But its eyes — two burning coals of malevolent red were terrifyingly clear as they stared down at the family with predatory hunger.

Jake whimpered, burrowing his face against Lisa's side. She stood transfixed, unable to tear her gaze from the nightmarish apparition. Tom, summoning strength from some deep reserve, straightened and moved to shield his family once more.

"Get in the car," he commanded, his voice barely above a whisper. "Now."

They scrambled to obey as the entity in the window unhinged its jaw, stretching its maw to impossible proportions. An unearthly wail split the night, a sound of such primordial terror that it seemed to curdle the very air.

Lisa's fingers, numb with fear, fumbled with the keys. The small piece of metal slipped and danced in her grasp as if possessed by its own malicious will. With a desperate cry, she managed to press the button, the sound of the locks disengaging like a starting pistol in their race for survival.

"Get in!" Tom's voice cracked like a whip as he all but hurled Emily and Jake into the backseat, their small bodies tumbling onto the leather. The door slammed shut with a finality that echoed in the night.

Lisa wrenched open the driver's side door, her movements frantic yet clumsy with fear. As she slid behind the wheel, some perverse instinct compelled her to look back at the house. The window gaped empty and dark, and the nightmarish visage vanished like a fever dream.

Tom threw himself into the passenger seat, his face a mask of urgency. "Go, go!"

The tires shrieked in protest as Lisa floored the accelerator, the car fishtailing out of the driveway in a spray of gravel. As they hurtled down the inky ribbon of country road, Lisa's eyes flicked constantly to the rearview mirror. She half-expected to see that hellish face materializing out of the darkness, giving chase. But there was only an impenetrable wall of night behind them, somehow more terrifying in its emptiness.

Minutes crawled by, the tense silence punctuated only by Jake's muffled sobs and the engine's desperate whine. Tom's voice, when it came, was low and grave. "We can't keep running forever. That...thing will just follow us."

Lisa's knuckles whitened on the steering wheel, her grip so tight she could feel the leather creaking. "So what do we do?" The question hung in the air, heavy with fear and uncertainty.

Tom reached over, placing a steadying hand on her arm. "I don't know," he admitted. "But I do know that if we keep running, we'll never be free. We have to face this— together."

A heavy silence fell over the car. Emily squirmed in her seat, the weight of her secret pressing down on her. She wanted to speak up, to confess, but the words stuck in her throat.

Finally, Lisa nodded, her expression a mixture of terror and determination. "Okay," she whispered. "Okay, we'll go back. God help us."

As Lisa slowly turned the car around, the family steeled themselves for the confrontation ahead. Unbeknownst to her parents, Emily silently vowed to find a way to undo her wish, to set things right—if only she could find the courage to tell them the truth.

CHAPTER 5
MALATHOR'S WELL

Lisa's eyes flew open, her heart pounding against her ribs. The darkness of the bedroom pressed in around her, thick and oppressive. Sweat beaded on her forehead as the remnants of her nightmare clung to her consciousness like cobwebs.

In her dream, she had stood at the edge of an ancient well, its stone walls slick with moss and decay. The forest around her had been unnaturally still, not even a whisper of wind disturbing the leaves. As she peered into the well's inky depths, a voice had risen from below, cold and ancient as the grave.

"The wish has been granted," it had hissed, the words seeming to coil around her like serpents. "A life must be given."

Lisa shuddered, the voice still echoing in her mind. She turned to Tom, shaking his shoulder urgently.

"Tom," she whispered, her voice quivering. "Tom, wake up."

He stirred, blinking in confusion. "Lisa? What's wrong?"

"I had a dream," she said, the words tumbling out in a rush. "About a well in the woods. It...it spoke to me."

As Lisa recounted her nightmare, a chill seemed to seep into the room. Tom sat up, his brow furrowed with concern. He opened his mouth to speak but froze as a shadow flickered across the wall, too fluid to be cast by the trees outside their window.

A quiet laugh drifted through the air, faint but unmistakable. It seemed to come from everywhere and nowhere at once.

"Did you hear that?" Tom whispered, his eyes wide.

Lisa nodded, her throat too tight for words. As one, they slipped out of bed and moved towards the children's room. The floorboards creaked beneath their feet, each sound amplified in the unnatural stillness of the house.

They found Emily first, her small form curled peacefully under her blankets, oblivious to the tension surrounding her. But when they reached Jake's bed, their hearts sank.

The boy was huddled in the corner, his knees drawn up to his chest, eyes wide and glassy in the dim light. He rocked back and forth, mumbling something under his breath.

"Jake?" Lisa called softly, taking a tentative step forward. "Sweetie, what's wrong?"

Jake looked up, his face a mask of terror. "It's here," he whispered. "The well. It's calling."

Lisa and Tom exchanged a look of helpless fear.

Jake's small hand trembled as he grasped Emily's wrist, pulling her into the shadowy corner of their playroom. His eyes, ringed with dark circles, darted nervously around the room before settling on his sister's face.

"Em," he whispered, his voice hoarse and quavering. "I need to tell you something. It's about the well."

Emily felt a chill run down her spine. "What about it?" she asked, trying to keep her voice steady.

Jake swallowed hard, his face pale and drawn. "It's angry, Em. The thing in the well...it's furious about your wish. I can hear it at night, whispering, demanding..." He trailed off, shuddering.

"Demanding what?" Emily pressed, her heart

pounding.

"Payment," Jake said, the word barely audible. "It wants payment for granting your wish."

Emily's stomach churned with guilt and fear. The memory of that day in the woods, of the coin dropping into the depths of the well, suddenly seemed sinister rather than magical.

"We have to tell Mom and Dad," she said, her voice shaking.

They found their parents in the living room, Lisa arranging flowers while Tom read the newspaper. The normalcy of the scene made Emily's task even harder.

"Mom, Dad," she began, her voice quavering. "I...I need to tell you something important."

Lisa and Tom looked up, concern etching their features as they noticed the children's distress.

Emily took a deep breath and began. "A few days ago, I found an old well in the woods behind our house. It had a sign that said, 'Be Careful What You Wish For.' I...I thought it was magical, so I made a wish. I wished for our family to be happy forever."

Her parents exchanged worried glances as Emily continued, her words tumbling out faster now. "I tossed a coin into the well when I made the wish. I heard a strange voice, but I thought I was imagining things. I'm so sorry. I didn't know it would cause trouble."

As Emily recounted her discovery of the well and the wish she'd made, the atmosphere in the room seemed to shift. The air grew heavy, charged with an unseen energy.

"I'm so sorry," Emily choked out, tears welling in her eyes. "I didn't know... I didn't mean to —"

Her words were cut short as the lights in the room began to flicker violently. The bulbs buzzed and popped, casting erratic shadows across the walls. A gust of icy wind whipped through the room, scattering papers and upending vases despite all the windows being firmly shut.

Lisa let out a startled cry, reaching for Tom's hand. Jake whimpered, pressing himself against Emily's side. The family huddled together in the center of the room, watching in horror as the supernatural manifestation continued around them.

As suddenly as it had begun, the wind died down, leaving the room in eerie silence. The lights stabilized but seemed dimmer than before as if some of their energy had been drained away.

Tom was the first to speak, his voice tight with suppressed fear. "We need to figure out what's going on. This...this isn't natural."

Lisa nodded, her arm protectively around Jake. "Whatever this is, whatever we've...awakened, we need to find a way to stop it. Before it's too late."

The family clung to each other, the weight of their situation settling over them like a shroud. They knew that they were facing something beyond their understanding, a supernatural threat that would require all their courage and resourcefulness to overcome.

As they began to discuss their next steps, none of them noticed the faint, sinister whisper that seemed to echo from the walls: "A life must be given..."

Lisa's fingers trembled as she flipped through the brittle pages of yet another dusty tome. The local library's archive room had become her second home over the past few days, its musty air and dim lighting a constant companion in her desperate search for answers.

"There has to be something here," she muttered,

squinting at the faded text of an old town record. Her eyes, red-rimmed from lack of sleep, widened as she stumbled upon a passage about the woods near their property.

"...and in the year 1692, three children of the township vanished without a trace. Last seen venturing into Willow Creek Forest, where whispers of an ancient well persist..."

Lisa's heart raced. She jotted down the information, adding it to her growing list of unsettling discoveries. Over the centuries, the forest had been a nexus of inexplicable events — disappearances, strange lights, eerie sounds that defied explanation.

As the sun began to set, casting long shadows through the archive's windows, Lisa gathered her notes and hurried home. She needed to share her findings with Tom and the children.

Meanwhile, across town, Tom sat in the cozy living room of Rose Harlow, their elderly neighbor and psychic medium. Emily and Jake huddled close to him on a floral-patterned sofa, their eyes wide as they watched Rose, her weathered hands clasped in her lap.

"The energy surrounding your family is...troubling," Rose murmured, her brow furrowed with concern. "There's a darkness, a presence that doesn't belong in this world. I've felt it growing stronger these past days."

Tom swallowed hard, tightening his grip on the children's shoulders. "Can you tell us more? What does it want?"

Rose's eyes flicked to Jake, lingering there with a look of worry. "The boy...the presence is strongest around him. There's a debt, a price that must be paid." She paused, her voice dropping to a whisper. "Be wary. What you've awakened is ancient and hungry. It's been waiting for so long."

As they left Rose's house, Tom's mind raced. He

ushered the children into the car, eager to get home and compare notes with Lisa.

The family reconvened in the living room as night fell, the atmosphere tense with anticipation. Lisa spread her research across the coffee table, pointing out the patterns she'd discovered.

"It's not just our well," she explained, her voice tight. "There's a history of strange occurrences in these woods going back centuries. Disappearances, unexplained phenomena—"

Tom nodded grimly. "Rose sensed something, too. She said there's a dark presence around us, especially Jake. She mentioned a debt—"

His words were cut short by a sound that made their blood run cold. A shriek, loud and inhuman, seemed to emanate from the very walls of the house. It was a sound of rage, of hunger, of something ancient and malevolent demanding its due.

The family huddled together, their faces pale in the dim light. The shriek faded, leaving behind a silence that felt oppressive and expectant.

"What do we do now?" Emily whispered, her voice trembling.

Lisa and Tom exchanged a look of determination tinged with fear. "We fight," Lisa said firmly. "Whatever this thing is, whatever it wants, we're not giving up without a fight."

As if in response, the lights flickered ominously, casting dancing shadows across the room. The battle against the well's sinister power had only just begun, and the Porter family knew that the stakes couldn't be higher.

CHAPTER 6
MALATHOR'S WELL

The kitchen basked in the warm, golden light of early morning, dust motes dancing in the sunbeams that streamed through the windows. The air was thick with the rich aroma of freshly brewed coffee, and the sweet scent of maple syrup drizzled over a stack of golden-brown pancakes. It was a deceptively normal morning, a fragile illusion of peace.

Jake sat hunched over his plate, his small frame seeming to shrink even further as he listlessly pushed his food around. The scrape of his fork against the ceramic created a discordant note in the otherwise peaceful kitchen symphony.

Lisa watched him with concern etched on her face, the lines around her eyes deepening. "Jake, honey, are you feeling okay?"

Before Jake could respond, his body went rigid. The fork slipped from his grasp, clattering against the hardwood floor with a sound that seemed to reverberate through the suddenly silent room. Jake's eyes, usually bright and full of life, rolled back, showing only whites against his rapidly paling skin.

"Jake?" Lisa's voice cracked, fear seeping into every syllable.

In what seemed like slow motion, Jake's small body went limp, slumping sideways in his chair. The scrape of chair legs against the floor was deafening as Lisa lunged forward, her coffee mug toppling and spilling a dark puddle across the table.

"Jake!" Lisa screamed, her arms encircling her son's limp form just before he hit the floor. Her voice was raw with panic as she called out, "Tom! Tom, help!"

Tom was already in motion, his chair toppling backward with a resounding crash. His hands shook as he fumbled for his phone, fingers slipping on the smooth surface. "I'm calling an ambulance," he said, his voice tight and strained, barely recognizable.

Lisa cradled Jake's unconscious form, her trembling hands brushing his sweat-dampened hair from his forehead. His skin felt clammy and cool to the touch, a stark contrast to the warm kitchen air. "Jake, baby, can you hear me? Please, wake up!" Her pleading words hung in the air, unanswered.

Emily stood frozen, her face a mask of shock, all color drained from her cheeks. Her voice, when it came, was a choked whisper. "Is...is he..."

"He's breathing," Lisa interrupted, her eyes never leaving Jake's face. She placed a hand on his chest, feeling the shallow rise and fall. "He's breathing, but he won't wake up. Tom, hurry!"

Tom's voice became a rushed blur in the background as he spoke to the emergency dispatcher, his words tumbling over each other in his haste. "Yes, my son, he just collapsed... No, he's not responding... Please, hurry!"

Emily took a hesitant step forward, the floorboard creaking under her weight. Her eyes were wide with a dawning horror, glistening with unshed tears. "It's my fault," she whispered, her voice barely audible over the sound of Tom's frantic phone call. "The wish...it's because of my wish..."

Lisa looked up, her face a complex mixture of fear, confusion, and disbelief. "Emily, no, this isn't—"

The wail of sirens in the distance cut her off, the sound

growing louder by the second, slicing through the morning calm. Tom rushed to the front door, the hinges groaning in protest as he flung it open. The flashing lights of the ambulance painted the walls in alternating shades of red and white, casting eerie, dancing shadows throughout the house.

The next few minutes were a whirlwind of activity. Paramedics flooded into the house, their voices a cacophony of calm yet urgent tones as they worked over Jake's still form. The acrid smell of antiseptic cut through the lingering breakfast aromas as they assessed Jake's condition. Lisa reluctantly let go of her son, her arms feeling achingly empty as they lifted him onto a stretcher. The wheels squeaked against the floor as they maneuvered through the narrow doorway.

As Jake was wheeled out, an eerie calm seemed to settle over the house. The air grew heavy and oppressive, almost expectant, as if the very walls were satisfied with this turn of events. The sudden silence was broken only by the soft ticking of the kitchen clock, each second punctuated by a quiet click that seemed to echo through the now-empty rooms.

Tom placed a hand on Lisa's shoulder, his touch gentle but firm. His voice was rough with emotion, barely above a whisper. "We need to go. We'll follow them to the hospital."

Lisa nodded numbly, reaching out to pull Emily close. The fabric of Emily's pajamas was soft under her trembling fingers. "It'll be okay," she murmured, though her voice lacked conviction. "Jake will be okay."

The family piled into their car, the leather seats cool against their skin. The silence was broken only by the sound of seat belts clicking into place and the engine roaring to life. As they pulled out of the driveway, following the ambulance's flashing lights, the weight of their situation was evident in their worried faces and tense postures. The early morning sun, once warm and comforting, now felt harsh and unforgiving as it glared through the windshield.

Emily stared out the window, her breath fogging the glass. Her voice was barely audible as she spoke, more to herself than anyone else. "I'm sorry," she whispered. "I'm so sorry."

No one responded. The only sound was the hum of the engine and the rhythmic thump of tires over the pavement as they sped towards the hospital, each lost in their own thoughts and fears about what was to come. The familiar streets of their neighborhood seemed alien and foreboding in the wake of the morning's events, a silent reminder that their world had irrevocably changed.

The drive was a blur, the small town's morning bustle a stark contrast to the stillness inside the car. Emily's whispered apologies echoed in their ears, a haunting refrain that underscored the gravity of their situation. As they approached the hospital, its towering structure loomed ahead, a beacon of both hope and despair.

As they hurried down the corridor, the harsh fluorescent lights of the hospital cast an unforgiving glare, deepening the shadows under Tom and Lisa's eyes. They now stood outside Jake's room, watching through the window as a nurse adjusted the various tubes and wires connected to their son's small, still form.

Dr. Martinez approached her face was a mask of professional concern. "Mr. and Mrs. Porter?"

Tom's head snapped up. "Yes? How is he?"

The doctor's brow furrowed. "Jake's condition is... unusual. His vital signs are stable, but we can't seem to wake him. It's not quite a coma, but..." She trailed off, clearly frustrated by the lack of answers.

"What does that mean?" Lisa asked, her voice tight with worry.

Dr. Martinez sighed. "Honestly, we're not sure. We're running more tests, but for now, all we can do is monitor him closely."

As the doctor walked away, Tom and Lisa exchanged a look heavy with unspoken fears. They moved closer to each other, their voices dropping to urgent whispers.

"Tom, this isn't natural," Lisa murmured, her eyes darting back to Jake's room. "First the well, then the noises in the house, and now this? It can't be a coincidence."

Tom ran a hand through his hair, his voice strained. "I know. God, I know. But what are we supposed to do? We can't exactly tell the doctors our son is in a supernatural coma because of a cursed well."

"It's my fault," came a small voice from behind them. They turned to see Emily huddled in a waiting room chair, her face pale and drawn. "I made the wish. I did this to Jake."

Lisa moved quickly to her daughter's side, kneeling in front of her. "No, sweetie. You didn't know. This isn't your fault."

But Emily shook her head, tears welling in her eyes. "But it is! If I hadn't made that stupid wish—"

"Stop," Tom said firmly, joining them. "We're going to figure this out. Together."

Lisa's eyes suddenly widened. "Wait. Remember Mrs. Harlow? The old woman who lives at the edge of town?"

Tom's expression shifted, recognition dawning. "Rose Harlow? The one I took the kids to see earlier?"

"Yes," Lisa nodded eagerly. "You said she seemed to know things—old stories about the town, unexplained events. Maybe she knows something more about the well."

"You think she could help?" Tom asked, skepticism warring with desperate hope in his voice.

Lisa glanced back at Jake's room, where the steady

beep of monitors provided a grim soundtrack. "At this point, what do we have to lose?"

Emily looked up, a tiny spark of hope in her tear-filled eyes. "Can we really help Jake?"

Tom and Lisa shared a determined look. "We're sure going to try," Tom said, squeezing Emily's hand. "We're not giving up on your brother."

———

Lisa's knuckles were white as she gripped the steering wheel, navigating the winding road that led to the outskirts of town. The sun was setting, casting long shadows across the pavement, as she pulled up to a weathered Victorian house that seemed to belong to another era entirely.

For a moment, Lisa sat in her car, doubt creeping in. Was she really going to consult a psychic about her son's condition? But as she thought of Jake lying motionless in the hospital bed, she steeled herself and got out of the car.

The porch steps creaked under her feet as she approached the front door. Before she could knock, it swung open, revealing a petite, elderly woman with silver hair and piercing blue eyes.

"Lisa Porter," the woman said, her voice surprisingly strong. "I've been expecting you. Come in, dear."

Lisa blinked in surprise. "Mrs. Harlow? I'm sorry, I didn't call ahead—"

Rose waved a hand dismissively. "No need for that. I knew you'd be coming. Please, call me Rose."

Lisa followed Rose into a cluttered living room filled with mismatched furniture and shelves overflowing with books and curios. The air was heavy with the scent of incense and old paper.

"Sit, dear," Rose said, gesturing to an overstuffed armchair. "Would you like some tea?"

Lisa shook her head. "No, thank you. I... I need your help, Mrs.—Rose. It's about my son, Jake."

Rose's eyes softened. "Yes, I know. Tom brought the children to see me earlier. But things have gotten worse, haven't they?"

The dam broke, and Lisa found herself pouring out the whole story—Emily's wish, the strange occurrences in their house, and finally, Jake's inexplicable coma. Rose listened intently, her expression growing more serious with each passing moment.

As Lisa finished speaking, she noticed the room seemed to have gotten darker, though she couldn't remember seeing Rose light any lamps. The old woman's face was grave in the dim light.

"I was afraid of this," Rose said softly. "The well you speak of...it's not just an old wishing well. It's much, much worse."

Lisa leaned forward, her heart pounding. "What do you mean? Do you know something about it?"

Rose nodded slowly. "Oh yes, I know its history. It's a cursed thing, that well. Created centuries ago by a witch of considerable power and malice."

"A witch?" Lisa's voice was barely a whisper.

"Indeed," Rose continued, her eyes taking on a faraway look. "She used it to collect sacrifices for the demon, Malathor. You see, the well doesn't just grant wishes. It demands payment—a life for a wish."

Lisa felt the blood drain from her face. "A life? But... Emily only wished for our family to be happy. How could that—"

"Happiness, wealth, love—the wish doesn't matter," Rose interrupted, shaking her head. "The well twists everything. It grants the wish, yes, but always at a terrible price. And now, I fear it's chosen Jake as its payment."

Lisa's hands trembled in her lap. "How do we stop it? There has to be a way to save Jake!"

Rose reached out, patting Lisa's hand gently. "There might be, dear. But it won't be easy, and it will be dangerous. Are you prepared for that?"

Lisa met Rose's gaze, her jaw set with determination. "I'll do anything to save my son. Anything."

The old woman nodded, a glimmer of respect in her eyes. "Then listen carefully. To break the well's curse, we'll need to perform a ritual at the site of the well itself."

Lisa leaned forward, hanging on every word.

Rose continued, her voice low and intense. "The ritual must be performed at midnight on the night of the new moon. You'll need to bring four items: something of great personal value, a lock of Jake's hair, a vial of water from the well itself, and..." She paused, her eyes clouding with worry.

"And what?" Lisa pressed.

Rose sighed heavily. "And blood freely given by the one who made the wish."

Lisa's breath caught in her throat. "Emily's blood? But she's just a child!"

"I know, dear. I know it sounds terrible," Rose said, her voice gentle but firm. "But it needn't be much. Just a few drops will do. The important thing is that it must be given willingly."

Lisa nodded slowly, her mind reeling. "What do we do with these items?"

"You'll need to create a circle around the well using salt," Rose explained. "Place the items at the four cardinal points of the circle. Then, you must recite an incantation while pouring the well water back into the well."

"What's the incantation?" Lisa asked, her voice barely

above a whisper.

Rose reached for a dusty, leather-bound book on a nearby shelf. She opened it carefully, the pages crackling with age. "Here it is," she said, pointing to a passage written in spidery handwriting. "Memorize these words, Lisa. They're crucial."

Lisa leaned in, committing the strange, ancient words to memory.

"But be warned," Rose added, her tone grave. "The well won't give up easily. It will fight back and try to stop you. You may see terrifying visions and hear voices urging you to stop. You must not falter, no matter what happens. If the ritual is interrupted, the consequences could be...dire."

Lisa swallowed hard, fear and determination warring within her. "I understand. Is there anything else?"

Rose's eyes softened with sympathy. "Just one more thing, dear. The most important part. At the end of the ritual, someone must make a final wish. A wish to seal the well forever."

"That sounds simple enough," Lisa said, relief evident in her voice.

But Rose shook her head slowly. "It's not as easy as it sounds. The wish must come from a place of pure intent, with no desire for personal gain. And the one who makes it... they'll bear the weight of containing the well's power for the rest of their life."

Lisa's eyes widened as the implications sank in. "You mean..."

"Yes," Rose nodded solemnly. "Whoever makes that final wish will be bound to the well's power. They'll ensure it can never harm anyone again but at a great personal cost."

The room fell silent as Lisa absorbed this information. The shadows seemed to press in around them as if the very darkness was listening, waiting to see what she would decide.

Finally, Lisa straightened her shoulders, a look of fierce determination on her face. "If that's what it takes to save Jake and make sure this never happens to anyone else, then I'll do it. I'll make the final wish."

Rose reached out, clasping Lisa's hand in her own gnarled one. "You're a brave woman, Lisa Porter. But remember, you don't have to face this alone. Your family's strength together might be the key to overcoming the well's power."

Lisa nodded, feeling a glimmer of hope for the first time since Jake fell ill. "Thank you, Rose. For everything."

As Lisa stood to leave, Rose called out one last warning. "Be careful, dear. And hurry. The new moon is only three days away, and the well's hold on Jake will only grow stronger with time."

With a final nod of understanding, Lisa stepped out into the gathering darkness, her mind racing with plans for the ritual that would determine her family's fate.

———

The steady beep of the heart monitor was the only constant in the otherwise unsettling quiet of Jake's hospital room. Tom sat slumped in an uncomfortable chair, his eyes red-rimmed from lack of sleep. Emily perched on the edge of the bed, her small hand resting on Jake's arm.

"Dad?" Emily's voice was barely above a whisper. "When's Mom coming back?"

Tom checked his watch, suppressing a yawn. "Soon, sweetie. She said she had to talk to someone who might be able to help Jake."

As if triggered by Jake's name, the fluorescent lights overhead flickered, casting momentary shadows across the room. Tom straightened, looking around warily.

"Did you see that?" he asked.

Emily nodded, her eyes wide. "It's been happening a lot. And look—" She pointed to the monitor displaying Jake's vitals. The numbers suddenly spiked, heart rate and blood pressure shooting up before settling back to normal just as quickly.

Tom frowned, leaning closer to examine the readout. "That's not normal. I should get a nurse—"

"No!" Emily grabbed his arm. "Please don't leave. I don't want to be alone."

Tom hesitated, then nodded, settling back into his chair. "Alright. But if it happens again, I'm calling someone."

Emily turned back to Jake, her face etched with guilt and worry. She leaned in close, her voice a trembling whisper. "I'm so sorry, Jake. This is all my fault. But I promise, we're going to fix this. Somehow."

The lights flickered again, more violently this time. The medical equipment in the room whirred and beeped erratically.

"Emily, get back," Tom said sharply, standing up. But before he could move, Jake's eyes flew open.

For a split second, relief flooded through Tom. But it was quickly replaced by a bone-deep terror as he realized something was horribly wrong. Jake's eyes were completely black, bottomless pits that seemed to absorb all light.

"Jake?" Emily's voice quavered.

Jake's head turned towards her with an unnatural smoothness. When his mouth opened, the voice that emerged was not that of a young boy. It was ancient, cold, and filled with malice.

"Payment is due," the voice rasped, echoing strangely in the small room. "A life for a wish. The debt must be paid."

Tom lunged forward, grabbing Emily and pulling her

away from the bed. "You're not Jake," he growled, trying to keep his voice steady despite his fear. "What have you done with my son?"

The thing wearing Jake's face smiled, a twisted parody of the boy's usual grin. "Your son is mine now. Unless..."

"Unless what?" Emily cried, tears streaming down her face.

"Unless payment is made," the voice hissed. "A life freely given. Choose quickly. The well grows hungry."

Jake's body convulsed suddenly, his back arching off the bed. The monitors shrieked in alarm as his vitals went haywire. Then, as abruptly as it had started, it stopped. Jake's eyes closed, and he lay still once more, the steady beep of the heart monitor the only sign that he was still alive.

Tom and Emily stood frozen, clinging to each other in shock and terror. The oppressive silence was broken by the sound of running footsteps in the hallway as nurses responded to the monitor alarms.

"Dad?" Emily's voice was small and frightened. "What are we going to do?"

Tom tightened his arm around her shoulders, his eyes never leaving Jake's motionless form. "I don't know, sweetheart. But we're not giving up. We're going to fight this thing, whatever it is. Together."

As the medical staff burst into the room, Tom silently prayed that Lisa would return soon. They needed answers, and they were running out of time.

———

Lisa's footsteps echoed through the sterile hospital corridor as she ran, her heart pounding in her chest. The elevator had been too slow; she'd taken the stairs two at a time, Rose's words ringing in her ears.

As she rounded the corner to Jake's room, a cacophony

of alarms and shouts assaulted her. Through the open door, she saw Jake's small body convulsing violently on the bed, his eyes open but unseeing, pitch black from corner to corner.

"Jake!" she cried, rushing forward.

Tom's strong arms caught her just as two nurses pushed past, hurrying to Jake's bedside. "Lisa, wait," he said, his voice strained. "Something's...wrong with him."

"It's the well," Lisa panted, watching in horror as the nurses struggled to restrain Jake. "Tom, I know what's happening. We have to—"

A guttural, inhuman sound cut through the chaos. Jake's mouth opened impossibly wide, and the voice that emerged was ancient and full of malice. "A life for a wish," it rasped. "Pay the price or suffer the consequences."

One of the nurses stumbled back, her face pale with shock. "Doctor! We need a doctor in here, stat!"

Emily huddled in the corner, her eyes wide with terror. "Mom," she whimpered. "What's happening to Jake?"

Lisa broke free from Tom's grasp, moving to gather Emily in her arms. "It's okay, sweetie. We're going to fix this."

As more medical staff flooded the room, Lisa pulled Tom and Emily into the hallway. Her words tumbled out in a rush. "I spoke to Rose Harlow. She told me about the well and its history. It's an ancient curse, Tom. It grants wishes but demands a life in return."

Tom's face drained of color. "A life? You mean—"

Lisa nodded grimly. "It wants Jake. But there's a way to break the curse. We have to perform a ritual at the well on the night of the new moon."

"When's that?" Emily asked, her voice small but determined.

"Three days from now," Lisa replied. "Rose gave me instructions, but...it won't be easy. And it's dangerous."

Tom ran a hand through his hair, glancing back at Jake's room, where the commotion was slowly subsiding. "Do we have a choice?"

"We'll do it," Emily said firmly, surprising both her parents with her resolve. "We have to save Jake."

Lisa knelt down, meeting Emily's eyes. "Sweetie, there's something you need to know. The ritual...it requires a few drops of your blood. Freely given."

Emily paled but nodded. "If it'll save Jake, I'll do it."

Tom looked between them, confusion and fear warring on his face. "Lisa, what aren't you telling us?"

Lisa took a deep breath, Rose's final warning echoing in her mind. "Rose said...to break a curse, you must outsmart the curser. But she warned that dark magic always demands a price."

"What kind of price?" Tom asked, his voice hushed.

Before Lisa could answer, a doctor emerged from Jake's room, his face grave. "Mr. and Mrs. Porter? We've sedated Jake for now, but...I've never seen anything like this. His condition is deteriorating rapidly. If we can't stabilize him soon..."

He didn't need to finish the sentence. The implication hung heavily in the air.

Lisa straightened, a fierce determination settling over her. "We understand, doctor. Thank you for everything you're doing."

As the doctor walked away, the Porter family huddled closer together. Tom wrapped an arm around Lisa's shoulders while Emily pressed between them.

"So what do we do now?" Tom asked softly.

Lisa's gaze hardened as she looked towards Jake's room, where their son lay fighting for his life against an evil they were only beginning to understand.

"We prepare," she said. "We gather what we need for the ritual. And in three days, we face that well and whatever dark power it holds. We're saving our son, no matter what it takes."

Emily nodded solemnly. "We're going to outsmart it, right, Mom?"

Lisa managed a small smile, ruffling Emily's hair. "That's right, sweetie. Together."

As they stood united in the harsh fluorescent light of the hospital hallway, none of them spoke of the fear that gripped their hearts. The malevolent presence of the well seemed to loom over them, unseen but felt, its hunger for a life yet unsatisfied.

Tom squeezed Lisa's hand. "Whatever happens, we face it as a family."

Lisa nodded, drawing strength from their unity. But deep down, she couldn't shake the dread that came with Rose's warning. Dark magic always demands a price. And as she looked at her husband and daughter, she silently vowed that she would be the one to pay it if it came to that.

The race against time had begun.

CHAPTER 7
MALATHOR'S WELL

The Porters' station wagon rolled to a stop in front of their house, its headlights cutting through the evening gloom. Lisa killed the engine, and for a moment, the family sat in silence, the weight of the past few days settling over them like a shroud.

Tom was the first to move. He opened his door, the sound unnaturally loud in the quiet street. "I'll get Jake," he said, his voice hoarse with fatigue.

Lisa nodded, then turned to Emily in the backseat. "Sweetie, can you grab Jake's bag?"

Emily nodded mutely, her small face pinched with worry and guilt.

As they approached the front door, the night nurse who had followed them from the hospital spoke softly. "I'll need to set up his equipment in his room. Which way is it?"

Lisa fumbled with her keys, her hands shaking slightly. "Up the stairs, second door on the right," she managed.

The moment the door swung open, something changed. The air inside seemed to thicken, becoming almost syrupy. Tom staggered slightly as he crossed the threshold, cradling Jake's limp form in his arms.

"What's wrong?" Lisa asked, steadying him.

Tom shook his head, blinking rapidly. "I don't know. It's just...hard to breathe in here."

As they moved further into the house, shadows danced at the edges of their vision. Lisa gasped as a dark shape seemed to lunge at her from the corner, only to dissipate like smoke when she turned to face it fully.

Emily clutched Jake's bag to her chest, her eyes wide with fear. "Mom," she whispered, "the shadows are moving."

Lisa forced a smile, though her heart was racing. "It's just tricks of the light, sweetie. We're all very tired."

But even as she said it, she saw another shadow rear up behind Emily, its form grotesque and threatening. Lisa bit back a scream, not wanting to frighten her daughter further.

Tom's face was pale as he started up the stairs with Jake. Each step seemed to require immense effort, as if he were wading through invisible molasses.

The nurse followed, her professional demeanor slipping slightly as she glanced nervously around the unnaturally dark hallway.

In the living room, Emily suddenly burst into tears. "I'm sorry," she sobbed, addressing the writhing darkness around them. "I'm so sorry. I didn't mean for this to happen."

As if in response, the shadows seemed to intensify, growing darker and more menacing. The air grew even heavier, and Lisa found herself gasping for breath.

"It's okay, Emily," she managed, pulling her daughter close. "Everything's going to be okay."

But as she looked up at Tom, she saw her own terror reflected in his eyes. Whatever presence had taken hold of their home, it was clear that it was far from okay. And it was angry.

As night fell, the malevolent presence in the house seemed to grow stronger, seeping into the minds of each family member and twisting their perceptions into nightmarish visions.

Lisa lay in bed alone, her eyes wide open, afraid to sleep. The bedroom walls began to ripple and distort as if made of liquid. She blinked hard, hoping to dispel the illusion, but when she opened her eyes again, the walls had melted away entirely. In their place was a vast, dark void that seemed to stretch into infinity.

"Tom?" she whispered, reaching out for her husband, but he wasn't there.

From the darkness, pale, elongated hands emerged, reaching towards her with grasping fingers. Lisa recoiled, pressing herself against the headboard. The hands kept coming, multiplying, filling her vision. She could almost feel their cold touch on her skin.

"This isn't real," she muttered, squeezing her eyes shut. "This isn't real."

In his study, Tom hunched over his desk, trying to lose himself in work. He shuffled through a stack of papers, but something caught his eye. The text on the page seemed to shift and change. He blinked, focusing harder, and felt his blood run cold.

The document in his hand was an obituary. Lisa's name was at the top, followed by her date of death—tomorrow's date. With trembling hands, he lifted the next paper. Another obituary, this time for Emily. Then Jake. Then himself.

"No," he breathed, his voice barely audible. He swept the papers off the desk, but as they fluttered to the floor, each one transformed into a death notice for someone he loved.

In her room, Emily huddled under her blankets, trying to block out the sounds around her. But the whispers persisted, seeming to come from the very air itself.

"Your fault," they hissed. "Jake's dying because of you."

"I didn't mean to," Emily whimpered, pressing her hands over her ears.

She peeked out from under the covers and immediately

wished she hadn't. Shadowy figures loomed around her bed, their forms indistinct but unmistakably menacing. Their voices grew louder, more accusing.

"You made the wish. You brought this upon your family."

Emily buried her face in her pillow, sobbing quietly. "I'm sorry, Jake. I'm so sorry."

Throughout the house, the visions persisted, each one different yet sharing a common thread — the sense of impending doom, the futility of resistance. In every shadow, every whisper, every terrifying image, the message was clear: Malathor's power was absolute, and death was coming for them all.

———

Morning light filtered through the kitchen windows, casting a deceptively cheerful glow on the Porter family as they gathered for breakfast. Dark circles rimmed their eyes, a testament to the night's horrors, but they clung to routine like a lifeline.

Lisa poured cereal with shaking hands. "Did everyone sleep okay?"

Tom and Emily exchanged glances, neither willing to speak of their nightmares.

"Fine," Tom muttered, reaching for the coffee pot.

The sudden squeak of the faucet made them all jump. Water gushed out at full force, splattering against the sink.

"I didn't—" Tom started, but his words were drowned out by a horrific groaning from deep within the walls.

In an instant, chaos erupted. Every faucet in the house seemed to turn on at once, the collective roar of water overwhelming. The kitchen sink overflowed in seconds, sending a torrent across the floor.

"What's happening?" Emily cried, scrambling onto a

chair as water soaked her socks.

Lisa yanked open a drawer, grabbing dish towels. "Tom, the main valve—"

Her words cut off in a gasp as water began seeping through the ceiling, forming impossible rivulets that defied gravity. It oozed from the walls, bubbling up between cracks in the floorboards.

Tom sloshed through the rising water towards the basement door, but the handle refused to budge. "It's stuck!" he shouted, shoulder slamming against the wood.

Emily stood transfixed, staring at the kitchen sink. The water churned, no longer simply overflowing but seeming to reach out, tendrils coiling in the air. She took a step forward, drawn by an irresistible pull.

"Emily, don't—" Lisa lunged for her daughter but slipped on the wet floor.

The water surged, forming a liquid hand that grasped Emily's arm. She didn't cry out, didn't resist, her eyes glassy and unfocused.

"Emily!" Tom's shout broke through her trance. She blinked, sudden terror flooding her face as she realized her predicament.

"Daddy! Help!"

Tom and Lisa scrambled towards her, fighting against the tide that threatened to sweep them off their feet. The watery grip was impossibly strong, dragging Emily closer to the sink's maw.

"Hold on, sweetie!" Lisa grabbed Emily's other arm, planting her feet against the cabinet for leverage. Tom wrapped his arms around both of them, straining backward.

For a moment, they were locked in a tug-of-war against a force of nature—or something far more sinister. The water pulsed, its grip tightening, intent on claiming its prize.

Emily's feet slipped on the wet floor, inching her closer to the sink. "It wants me," she whimpered. "The well wants me!"

"We've got you," Tom grunted, muscles straining. "We won't let go. Never."

With a final, desperate heave, they wrenched Emily free. The family tumbled backward, splashing into the knee-deep water that now filled the kitchen.

As suddenly as it began, the deluge ceased. Faucets sputtered and fell silent. Water drained away with unnatural speed, leaving the kitchen a dripping mess—but then blessedly dry.

They sat there, soaked and panting, clinging to each other. The morning sun continued to shine as if nothing had happened. But they all knew the truth. This was more than a freak plumbing accident. It was a message, a display of power.

Malathor had reached into their home, and it had nearly taken their daughter.

Emily broke the silence, her voice small and frightened. "I'm sorry. This is all my fault."

Lisa pulled her close, meeting Tom's eyes over their daughter's head. The same fear reflected in both their gazes.

"We'll figure this out," Tom said, trying to sound more confident than he felt. "Together."

But as Lisa looked around at their violated home, she couldn't shake the feeling that they were running out of time.

Suddenly, the air filled with whispers, faint at first but quickly growing in volume. The family huddled closer, straining to understand the cacophony of voices that seemed to come from everywhere and nowhere at once.

"What's it saying?" Emily whimpered, hands pressed over her ears.

Tom shook his head, eyes darting around the room. "I

can't—"

The whispers crescendoed, becoming clear enough to understand. "Ancient pacts must be honored," they hissed. "The price of wishes must be paid."

"Leave us alone!" Lisa shouted, but her voice was drowned out by the otherworldly chorus.

"Malathor's victory is inevitable," the voices intoned, growing louder still. "A life for a wish. The bargain must be kept."

The kitchen erupted into chaos. Cabinet doors flew open, dishes and utensils launching into the air as if caught in a whirlwind. A fork whizzed past Tom's ear, embedding itself in the wall behind him.

"Get down!" he yelled, trying to shield Emily and Lisa with his body.

The water surged again, rising rapidly around their ankles. Emily screamed as she felt the cold grip on her leg, trying to drag her down.

"No!" Lisa cried, grabbing for her daughter.

Pots and pans clanged against each other in midair, creating a deafening metallic symphony that mixed with the roar of water and the relentless whispers. A heavy cast iron skillet struck Tom's shoulder, nearly causing him to lose his grip on Emily.

"Dad!" Emily gasped, terror etched on her face as the water pulled harder.

In that moment, something changed in Emily's eyes. Fear gave way to determination, a spark of defiance igniting within her. With a strength that surprised even herself, she planted her free foot firmly on the ground.

"No," she said, her voice quiet but firm. Then louder: "No!"

The whispers faltered for a split second, and Emily

seized the moment. She took a deep breath and, in a voice clear and strong that belied her young age, she shouted: "Malathor, leave my family alone!"

The effect was instantaneous. The kitchen fell into an eerie, sudden silence. The whirlwind of objects stopped as if a switch had been flipped, dishes and utensils clattering to the ground. The water receded with a speed that defied physics, draining away in the blink of an eye.

For a long moment, the Porter family stood frozen, hardly daring to breathe. The only sound was the drip-drip-drip of water from the soaked surfaces of their kitchen.

Emily stood at the center of it all, her small frame radiating an unexpected power. She looked around, a mix of surprise and relief on her face.

"Is...is it over?" she asked, her voice now small again.

Tom pulled her into a tight hug, wincing slightly from his injured shoulder. "I don't know, sweetie. But that was... that was amazing."

Lisa joined the embrace, her eyes wide with a mix of pride and lingering fear. "How did you do that, Emily?"

Emily shook her head, looking as confused as her parents. "I don't know. I just...I just knew I had to make it stop."

As the family held each other in the aftermath of the supernatural assault, a new feeling permeated the air—a glimmer of hope. For the first time since this nightmare began, they had fought back. And for a moment, at least, they had won.

But in the back of their minds, a nagging doubt remained. Was this truly over, or merely a temporary reprieve? The silence that now enveloped their home felt not like peace but like the calm before an even greater storm.

Their relief was short-lived. As they began to

disentangle themselves from their group hug, a deep, menacing laugh reverberated through the house. It started low, almost subsonic, rattling the dishes that lay scattered on the floor. Then it grew, filling every corner of the kitchen with its malevolent mirth.

"What's happening?" Emily whimpered, clinging tighter to her parents.

Tom's eyes darted around the room, searching for the source of the laughter. "I don't know, but stay close."

The shadows in the corners of the kitchen began to writhe and twist, stretching across the floor and walls like living ink. They converged in the center of the room, coalescing into a towering, humanoid figure that loomed over the huddled family.

Lisa gasped, instinctively pushing Emily behind her. "Oh my God," she breathed.

The shadow figure seemed to absorb all light around it, its edges shimmering with an otherworldly energy. Though it had no discernible face, the family could feel its gaze upon them, cold and ancient and hungry.

When it spoke, its voice seemed to come from everywhere at once, reverberating in their heads and in the air around them. "Your resistance is admirable," it said, the words slithering into their ears, "but futile."

Tom stood straighter, placing himself between the entity and his family. "Who are you? What do you want?"

The shadow rippled, almost like a chuckle. "I am Malathor, keeper of the well, granter of wishes." Its attention seemed to focus on Emily. "And collector of debts."

Emily shrank back, her earlier bravery faltering in the face of this manifestation.

"The wish has been granted," Malathor continued, its voice growing harder, more insistent. "And payment must be made. A life for a wish — that is the law of ancient magic."

"No," Lisa said, shaking her head frantically. "We never agreed to this. We didn't know!"

"Ignorance does not negate the pact," Malathor replied, implacable. "The wish was made, the coin was cast. Balance must be restored."

The temperature in the room plummeted, their breaths coming out in visible puffs. The shadow expanded, tendrils of darkness creeping towards them.

"Choose," Malathor commanded. "Choose who will pay the price, or I shall choose for you."

Tom's face paled as the full implication of the ultimatum sank in. "You can't expect us to...to sacrifice one of us. That's inhuman!"

A sound like a grinding stone filled the air — Malathor's approximation of laughter. "Human concerns are irrelevant. The magic demands payment."

Emily stepped forward, tears streaming down her face. "This is my fault. I made the wish. I should — "

"No!" Lisa and Tom cried in unison, pulling her back.

"We won't let you have her," Lisa said, her voice shaking but determined. "We won't let you have any of us."

The shadow loomed closer, its voice dropping to a bone-chilling whisper. "Then you have made your choice. I shall claim what is owed, and your suffering will be legendary."

The family huddled together, clinging to each other as the shadow of Malathor stretched over them. The true horror of Emily's innocent wish now lay bare before them, a nightmare made real, with no apparent way out.

As darkness enveloped them, one thought echoed in their minds: How could they possibly survive this?

CHAPTER 8
MALATHOR'S WELL

Darkness fell early, surrendering to a long night pregnant with foreboding. Inside the Porter home, an atmosphere of grim determination reigned as the family made their final preparations.

Lisa stood in the living room, a crumpled piece of paper clutched in her trembling hands. Her eyes moved over the words of the incantation, again and again, committing each syllable to memory. She looked up as Tom entered the room, his face a mask of worry and resolve.

"Did you get everything Rose told us to bring?" Lisa asked, her voice barely above a whisper.

Tom nodded, patting the satchel slung over his shoulder. "It's all here. The lock of Jake's hair, the vial of water from the well..." He swallowed hard, his hand moving to his chest where, beneath his shirt, hung the St. Christopher medal his father had given him years ago. "And something of great personal value."

Lisa's hand instinctively went to her wrist, where she wore the charm bracelet her grandmother had left her. "I've got mine too." Her eyes darted to the clock on the wall. "It's almost midnight. The new moon is high, just like Rose said it needed to be."

"What about the fourth item?" Emily's small voice came from the doorway. She stood there, clutching a worn teddy bear—the one she'd had since she was a baby. "Rose said we needed four things, right?"

Tom and Lisa exchanged a pained look. Rose's words echoed in their minds: "And the fourth item...it must be freely given, with full understanding of the consequences. A drop of blood from an innocent."

Lisa knelt down beside Emily, gently stroking her hair. "Sweetie, we've talked about this. You don't have to—"

"I want to," Emily interrupted, her voice stronger than before. "I made the wish. I have to help make it right."

Tom sighed heavily, then nodded. "Alright. But we'll do that part at the well, okay? For now, let's focus on getting there."

Lisa stood, taking a deep breath to steady herself. "It's time, then."

As one, the Porter family moved to the front door. Tom reached for the handle, then paused, looking back at his wife and daughter. "Whatever happens out there...I love you both. So much."

"I love you too," Lisa and Emily replied in near-unison.

With a nod, Tom opened the door, and they stepped out into the night.

The cold hit them immediately, a biting wind that cut through their jackets and seemed to chill them to the bone. Their breaths plumed in the frigid air, small clouds of warmth quickly swallowed by the darkness. The usual sounds of a winter evening—the distant scrape of snow shovels, the muffled bark of a neighbor's dog—were conspicuously absent. An unnatural silence blanketed the neighborhood, broken only by the crunch of snow under their feet as they made their way down the driveway.

As they turned towards the woods, the air seemed to thicken, becoming almost syrupy despite the cold. Each breath felt labored, as if the very atmosphere was trying to hold them back.

Emily's lantern bobbed gently as they walked, the only point of warmth in a world that felt colder and darker than any winter night they'd known. The trees loomed ahead, their bare branches reaching out like gnarled fingers, beckoning them deeper into the forest.

Lisa shivered, pulling her coat tighter around herself. "It knows we're coming," she murmured.

Tom nodded grimly. "Good. Let it know. We're not sneaking in — we're here to end this."

As they reached the edge of the woods, they paused for a moment. The path ahead was dark, the trees pressing close on either side. Somewhere in those woods, Malathor's well waited for them, ancient and malevolent.

Emily's small hand found Lisa's, squeezing tight. "I'm scared," she admitted.

"Me too, sweetie," Lisa replied, surprised by the steadiness in her own voice. "But we're going to face this fear together."

Tom took a deep breath, his exhale forming a thick cloud in the frigid air. "For Jake," he said softly.

Lisa nodded. "For Jake. For all of us."

With one last look at each other, the Porter family stepped off the snowy sidewalk and onto the forest path. As the trees closed in around them, nature seemed to hold its breath, waiting to see what the long winter night would bring.

The forest path, once familiar, had transformed into a gauntlet of supernatural horrors. Tom took the lead, his breath coming in ragged gasps as he hacked through the unnaturally thick undergrowth with a machete. Each swing revealed more tangled vegetation as if the forest itself was trying to bar their way.

"Stay close," he called over his shoulder, his voice tense.

Lisa gripped Emily's hand tightly, her other arm wrapped protectively around her daughter's shoulders. "We're right behind you," she assured him, though her eyes darted nervously from shadow to shadow.

A root suddenly sprang up from the ground, catching Tom's foot. He stumbled, barely catching himself before he fell.

"Dad!" Emily cried out.

"I'm okay," Tom grunted, regaining his footing. "Just... watch your step. The ground's not what it seems."

As they pressed on, the trees seemed to press closer, their branches reaching out like gnarled fingers. Lisa yelped as a branch whipped across her cheek, leaving a thin scratch.

"Mom?" Emily's voice quavered.

"It's nothing, sweetie," Lisa said, forcing a smile. "Just a scratch."

The wind picked up, carrying with it whispers that seemed to come from everywhere and nowhere at once. Unintelligible at first, they gradually became clearer, more menacing.

"Turn back," they hissed. "You don't belong here."

"Save yourselves," others warned. "Before it's too late."

Emily whimpered, pressing closer to her mother. "I don't like this," she whispered.

"I know, honey," Lisa soothed, though her own heart was racing. "But we have to keep going. For Jake, remember?"

Emily nodded, straightening her shoulders. "For Jake," she echoed.

As they ventured deeper into the woods, a thick fog began to roll in, obscuring the path ahead. It curled around their ankles, cold and clammy, making each step treacherous.

"Tom?" Lisa called out, barely able to see her husband

a few feet ahead.

"Still here," he answered, his voice tight with concentration. "Just...just keep following the sound of my voice."

Suddenly, a figure darted between the trees to their right. Emily gasped, pointing. "Did you see that?"

Before Lisa could answer, another spectral form flitted past on their left, accompanied by a burst of hollow, chilling laughter.

"Oh God," Lisa breathed, pulling Emily closer.

The ghostly figures continued to dance at the edge of their vision, always just out of clear sight. Their laughter grew louder, more mocking, sending shivers down the family's spines.

"Don't look at them," Tom ordered, his voice strained but determined. "They're not real. They can't hurt us."

But even as he spoke, a branch swung down from above, nearly striking him. He ducked just in time, the wood whistling past his ear.

"Tom!" Lisa cried out.

"I'm okay," he assured her, though his voice shook slightly. "We're close now. We have to be."

Emily stumbled, and Lisa quickly steadied her. "You all right, sweetie?"

Emily nodded, her face pale but resolute in the lantern light. "I'm scared, Mom," she admitted. "But...but I won't let Jake down. We have to keep going."

Lisa felt a surge of pride through her fear. "That's my brave girl," she said, squeezing Emily's hand.

Tom paused for a moment, turning back to his family. Despite the scratches on his face and the weariness in his eyes, his gaze was full of love and determination.

"We're in this together," he reminded them. "Whatever

happens, we face it as a family."

Lisa nodded, meeting his eyes. "As a family," she agreed.

With renewed resolve, they pressed on through the hostile forest, each step bringing them closer to Malathor's well and the confrontation that awaited them. The woods might be against them, filled with terrors both seen and unseen, but the Porters had something stronger on their side — their love for each other and their unwavering determination to save Jake.

As they pushed through another cluster of grasping branches, a clearing began to take shape ahead, barely visible through the fog. And there, at its center, loomed the dark silhouette of the well.

The Porters stumbled into the clearing, their breath coming in ragged gasps. For a moment, they simply stood there, staring at the source of their nightmares.

Malathor's well, once an innocent-looking structure overgrown with vines, had transformed into something utterly alien. It pulsed with an eerie energy, dark tendrils of power visibly emanating from its depths like writhing tentacles.

Tom swallowed hard, then turned to Lisa. "What did Rose say we need to do first?"

Lisa nodded, steeling herself. "We need to create a circle around the well using salt," she said, her voice shaky but determined. "Then place the items at the four cardinal points."

"Right," Tom said, reaching into his satchel. He pulled out a container of salt and handed it to Lisa. "You start the circle. Emily and I will get the items ready."

As Lisa began to pour the salt in a wide circle around the well, Tom and Emily carefully laid out their precious cargo: Jake's lock of hair to the north, Tom's St. Christopher medal to the east, Lisa's charm bracelet to the south, and Emily's teddy bear with her precious drop of blood to the west.

"Now what?" Emily asked, her voice small but steady.

Lisa took a deep breath. "Now I recite the incantation while pouring the well water back into the well."

She took a tentative step forward, withdrawing the crumpled paper and the vial of well water from her pocket. The words, carefully memorized, suddenly seemed to swim before her eyes. Lisa closed her eyes for a moment, centering herself, then began to read.

"By the power of earth and sky," she intoned, her voice growing stronger with each word, "by the strength of love and sacrifice..."

As she spoke, she uncorked the vial and began to pour its contents back into the well. The reaction was immediate and violent.

Malathor appeared before them. "FOOLISH MORTALS," it boomed, the words reverberating through their bones. "YOU KNOW NOT WHAT FORCES YOU TAMPER WITH."

Tom stepped forward, placing himself between the entity and his family. "We know enough," he said, his voice steady despite his fear. "We're here to end this."

The fiery pinpricks of Malathor's eyes flared brighter. "END THIS? OH, BUT WE'VE ONLY JUST BEGUN." Its tone shifted, becoming almost gentle, seductive. "THERE IS NO NEED FOR CONFLICT. I CAN BE GENEROUS. I CAN GRANT YOUR HEART'S DESIRES."

The shadowy form rippled, and suddenly, an image appeared within it—Jake, healthy and smiling. Emily gasped.

"YOUR SON CAN BE SAVED," Malathor crooned. "ALL I ASK IN RETURN IS WHAT IS RIGHTFULLY MINE." Its gaze fixed on Emily. "THE ONE WHO MADE THE WISH.

A FAIR EXCHANGE, IS IT NOT?"

"No!" Lisa cried, pulling Emily close. "Never!"

Malathor's form darkened. "THEN PERHAPS A DIFFERENT BARGAIN." It turned to Tom. "THINK OF IT, THOMAS. SUCCESS BEYOND YOUR WILDEST DREAMS. WEALTH. POWER. ALL CAN BE YOURS." The shadow rippled again, showing visions of Tom in expensive suits, in boardrooms, in mansions. "ALL IT WOULD COST IS ONE LIFE." Its gaze shifted to Lisa.

Tom's face contorted with rage. "Go to hell," he spat.

Throughout this psychological assault, Lisa had been muttering under her breath, her voice growing stronger with each passing moment. "...by the bonds of family, by the strength of love freely given..."

Malathor's form convulsed. "SILENCE, WITCH!" it roared. "YOU KNOW NOT WHAT YOU DO!"

But Lisa pressed on, her voice rising. "We reject your false promises. We deny your claim!"

Realizing the danger, Malathor unleashed its full fury upon them. Tom cried out, clutching his chest as phantom pain lanced through him. Emily screamed, pointing at horrors only she could see lurking at the edge of the clearing. Lisa choked and gasped, feeling as if she were drowning despite the dry land beneath her feet.

Yet they fought on. Tom, through gritted teeth, reached out to steady Lisa. "Keep...keep going," he managed. "We're with you."

Emily, tears streaming down her face, hugged her mother's legs. "You can do it, Mom," she sobbed. "Don't let it win."

Lisa's voice faltered as she struggled for breath, but she forced the words out. "By...by the light that shines in darkness..."

Malathor howled, its form writhing in fury. The attacks intensified. Tom fell to his knees, his face pale with pain. Emily wailed as nightmarish visions assaulted her. Lisa felt icy water filling her lungs.

But still, they endured. Tom, on his knees, pulled himself to Lisa's side, supporting her. Emily, eyes squeezed shut against the horrors around her, clung to her parents.

"Together," Tom gasped. "We do this together."

Lisa nodded, gathering her strength. She looked at her husband, battered but unbowed. At her daughter, terrified but brave. Drawing strength from their love, she raised her voice, clear and strong, to continue the counter-spell.

As she spoke, a warm light began to emanate from the three of them, pushing back against Malathor's darkness. The entity's attacks grew more frenzied but less effective as the family stood united against its onslaught.

Lisa's voice grew stronger as she neared the end of the incantation. The warm light emanating from the family pulsed brighter, pushing back against Malathor's writhing darkness. But as she spoke the penultimate line, her voice faltered.

"Mom?" Emily called out, worry clear in her voice.

Lisa turned to her family, her eyes shimmering with tears and determination. "I know what I have to do," she said softly. "It's the only way to end this, to save you both and Jake."

Realization dawned on Tom's face. "Lisa, no!" he shouted, reaching for her. "You can't!"

"I have to," Lisa insisted, taking a step towards the well. "A life for a wish. That's what it wants. That's what it's always wanted."

Emily lunged forward, grabbing her mother's arm. "No, Mom! Please!" she sobbed. "There has to be another way!"

Lisa gently cupped Emily's face. "I'm so sorry, sweetie. I love you so much. Both of you. Tell Jake I love him too."

"Lisa, don't do this!" Tom pleaded, his voice breaking. "We'll find another way. Together!"

But Lisa's mind was made up. She turned back to the well, where Malathor's form churned with dark anticipation. She took a deep breath and stepped forward.

In that moment, something shifted in Emily's eyes. A look of sudden understanding, of clarity beyond her years, passed over her face. Without warning, she darted forward and snatched the paper with the spell from her mother's hand.

"Emily, what are you—" Lisa began, but Emily's voice, suddenly ringing with power and love, drowned her out.

"By the power of truth and love," Emily proclaimed, her young voice carrying an authority that belied her age, "I renounce the wish I made and all the fortune it brought!"

Malathor's form convulsed, a sound like shattering glass emanating from its core. "NO!" it howled, its voice losing its otherworldly resonance. "YOU CANNOT—"

But Emily pressed on, her voice growing stronger. "I offer not a life but the undoing of what was done. I choose love over fortune, family over fate!"

The clearing erupted into chaos. Malathor's form began to lose cohesion. Parts of it sucked back into the well like smoke drawn into a vacuum. It thrashed and wailed, its cries a mixture of rage and confusion.

"You dare?" it shrieked, its voice now almost human in its desperation. "You cannot undo what has been done!"

"I can," Emily stated, her voice calm amidst the maelstrom. "And I do."

Lisa and Tom watched in awe as their daughter stood firm, the paper with the spell clutched in her small hand, facing down the ancient entity. The warm light that had surrounded them now coalesced around Emily, growing brighter with each word she spoke.

Malathor's form continued to disintegrate, drawn inexorably back into the well. Its howls of rage turned to screams of despair as Emily's pure intention counteracted its dark magic.

"This isn't over!" it wailed, its voice fading. "You cannot escape the price—"

Its final words were cut off as a blinding flash of light erupted from the well, so bright that the Porters had to shield their eyes. A sound like stone cracking echoed through the clearing, followed by a thunderous boom.

And then, silence. Complete and absolute.

Slowly, tentatively, the Porters lowered their arms, blinking spots from their vision. The well stood before them, no longer pulsing with dark energy but looking old and weathered—and with a large crack running down its side.

For a long moment, no one moved. Then, as one, they came together, clinging to each other tightly. Lisa enveloped Emily in a fierce hug while Tom wrapped his arms around them both.

"Is it...is it over?" Emily whispered, her voice once again that of a young girl, tired and scared.

Tom and Lisa exchanged a look over her head. In Lisa's eyes, Tom saw his own mixture of hope and uncertainty reflected.

"I don't know, sweetie," Lisa answered honestly. "But whatever happens next, we'll face it together."

As they stood there, holding each other in the silent clearing, the first light of dawn began to peek through the trees. Whether they had truly won or merely angered an ancient evil remained to be seen. But for now, they were together, they were alive, and they had hope.

And sometimes, that's enough to face whatever comes next.

CHAPTER 9
MALATHOR'S WELL

The quiet of Jake's bedroom was suddenly broken by a chorus of electronic beeps. The medical equipment surrounding his bed sprang to life, screens flickering with a flurry of new data. Lisa Porter's head snapped up from where it had been resting on Tom's shoulder, her eyes wide with a mixture of hope and trepidation.

"Tom," she whispered, gripping his arm. "Look!"

They leaned forward in their chairs, scarcely breathing as Jake's eyelids fluttered. For a heart-stopping moment, nothing happened. Then, with a sudden, violent motion, Jake's eyes flew open. He sucked in a deep, ragged breath, his small chest heaving as if he'd just broken the surface after a long dive.

"Jake!" Lisa cried, rushing to the bedside. Tom was right behind her, his face a mask of disbelief and joy.

Jake blinked rapidly, his gaze darting around the familiar surroundings of his room, now cluttered with medical equipment. "Mom?" he croaked, his voice hoarse from disuse. "Dad? What...what's going on?"

Lisa couldn't speak through her tears. She reached out, cupping Jake's face in her trembling hands. Tom placed a steadying hand on her shoulder, his own eyes glistening.

"You're okay, buddy," Tom managed, his voice thick with emotion. "You haven't been feeling well, but you're going to be fine now."

Emily, who had been curled up in the reading nook

in their bedroom, scrambled to join her family. "Jake!" she exclaimed, reaching for her brother's hand. "You're awake!"

Jake's brow furrowed as he looked at each of their faces, then at the unfamiliar medical equipment surrounding his bed. "Why is all this stuff in my room? What happened?"

The Porters exchanged a quick, loaded glance over Jake's head. In that silent moment, a decision was made. Lisa smoothed Jake's hair back from his forehead, forcing a watery smile.

"Nothing for you to worry about, sweetheart," she said softly. "You just haven't been feeling well, but you're better now. That's all that matters."

As Jake settled back against his pillows, still looking bewildered but comforted by his family's presence, Tom met Lisa's eyes. They shared a look of profound relief tinged with lingering fear. The horrors they had faced, the nightmare they had endured—none of that would touch Jake. They would protect him from that darkness, no matter what.

In the days that followed, the Porter family fell into a rhythm of quiet normalcy. They spent their time together, sharing meals and laughter, carefully avoiding any mention of the hospital equipment still crowding Jake's room. Lisa and Tom took turns staying by Jake's side, answering his questions with half-truths and comforting lies. The relief they felt was palpable, but so was the fear—the fear of what could have been and what might still be.

The Porter house stood quiet in the pale morning light, its inhabitants moving through their routines like actors in a play they'd forgotten the lines to. Lisa stood at the kitchen counter, mechanically spreading peanut butter on bread for the kids' lunches. Her gaze drifted to the window, where her easel sat abandoned in the corner of the yard, a half-finished canvas slowly weathering in the elements.

Tom entered, adjusting his tie with practiced motions. "I'm heading out," he said, his voice flat.

Lisa turned, forcing a smile that didn't reach her eyes. "Have a good day," she replied, the words sounding hollow even to her own ears.

Tom hesitated, then said, "I spoke with Mr. Hendricks yesterday. Told him I couldn't accept the promotion."

Lisa's eyes widened. "Tom, are you sure? That was such a big opportunity..."

He shook his head, a haunted look crossing his face. "It wasn't...it wasn't real, Lisa. None of it was. And even if it had been..." He trailed off, then finished quietly, "Some things are more important."

Lisa nodded, understanding all too well. She glanced at her own hands, remembering the feverish inspiration that had gripped her, the paintings that had sold for thousands. Now, she couldn't bear to lift a brush.

Emily trudged into the kitchen, her backpack dragging on the floor behind her. Gone was the skip in her step, the constant chatter about imaginary worlds and make-believe adventures.

"Morning, sweetie," Lisa said gently. "I made your favorite for lunch today."

Emily nodded solemnly. "Thanks, Mom," she said, her voice small. She paused, then asked, "Is it okay if I have apple slices instead of chips? I was thinking...too much salt isn't good for you."

Lisa and Tom exchanged a look, a mixture of sadness and concern passing between them. Their little girl, once so carefree, now weighed every decision with a gravity beyond her years.

"Of course, honey," Lisa said, reaching for an apple.

"That's very thoughtful of you."

As Emily sat at the table, nibbling half-heartedly at her breakfast, Jake's laughter drifted down from upstairs. The sound, once so commonplace, now felt like a miracle. Relief washed over Lisa and Tom, but it was tinged with a lingering unease. The joy of hearing their son's carefree giggles was profound, yet it also served as a stark reminder of how close they had come to losing him forever. Their smiles, though genuine, carried the weight of their recent ordeal, a complex mixture of gratitude and residual fear that they couldn't quite shake.

They had their son back, their family was whole, but the shadow of what they'd endured—what they'd almost lost—hung over them like a shroud. Every laugh seemed brittle, every moment of joy tinged with the fear that it could all be snatched away in an instant.

As Tom kissed Lisa goodbye and ruffled Emily's hair, his eyes met his wife's once more. In that glance was an unspoken agreement: they would get through this, somehow. They had to. For Jake, for Emily, for each other. But the road ahead was long, and the darkness they'd glimpsed wasn't easily forgotten.

The Porter's driveway buzzed with activity as the family loaded the last of their belongings into their overstuffed car. Tom grunted as he maneuvered a heavy box into the trunk while Lisa double-checked the straps securing their mattresses to the roof.

Emily stood on the front lawn, clutching her favorite stuffed animal and staring at the house with a mixture of sadness and relief. Jake, still a bit wobbly on his feet, sat on the front steps, watching the proceedings with wide eyes.

"Is that everything?" Lisa called out, wiping sweat

from her brow.

Tom nodded, slamming the trunk shut. "I think so. We can always come back if we've forgotten anything."

"No," Lisa said quickly, her voice tight. "We're not coming back. Whatever we left, it stays here."

A tense silence fell over the family, broken only by the sound of gravel crunching underfoot. They turned to see Rose Harlow approaching, her weathered face etched with concern.

"So, you're really leaving," Rose said, her eyes taking in the packed car and the family's drawn faces.

Tom nodded, stepping forward to shake her hand. "We are. After everything...we just can't stay."

Rose clasped his hand in both of hers, her grip surprisingly strong. "You're doing the right thing," she said, her voice low and earnest. "You've shown great courage, all of you. And wisdom, too, in knowing when to walk away."

Lisa joined them, wrapping an arm around Emily's shoulders. "We can't thank you enough for your help, Mrs. Harlow. We wouldn't have made it through without you."

Rose's eyes softened, but there was a glimmer of something else there — a warning. "You're welcome, dear. But remember..." She paused, glancing at each of them in turn. "Malathor may be defeated, but the power of wishes — and their consequences — remains a force in this world. Don't ever forget what you've learned here."

The Porters exchanged solemn looks, the weight of Rose's words settling heavily upon them. Even Jake, who didn't fully understand what had happened, seemed to sense the gravity of the moment.

Emily spoke up, her voice small but determined. "We won't forget, Mrs. Harlow. I promise."

Rose nodded, a sad smile tugging at her lips. "Good

girl. Now, go on. Your new life is waiting for you."

With a final, knowing nod, Rose turned and made her way back down the gravel path, her figure gradually dissolving into the morning mist. The Porters watched her go, each feeling the weight of her absence — their one true ally in the nightmare they'd endured, their bridge between the world they'd known and the dark mysteries they'd discovered.

The Porter family stood in their driveway, the car packed to bursting behind them. Their gazes were fixed on the house, once a symbol of new beginnings, now a repository of haunting memories.

Lisa exhaled slowly. "It feels wrong to just...drive away."

Tom nodded, his jaw tight. "I know what you mean."

Emily tugged at her mother's sleeve. "Can we...can we go see it? One last time?"

The adults exchanged a look of understanding. Even Jake, still pale and tired, seemed to perk up at the suggestion.

"Okay," Tom said finally. "One last visit."

They made their way down the now-familiar forest path, dappled sunlight playing across their faces. The woods seemed less oppressive in the daylight, yet an undercurrent of unease thrummed beneath their feet with each step.

As they entered the clearing, the well stood before them, looking deceptively ordinary — just an old stone structure wrapped in vines. But as they gathered around it, a collective shiver ran through the family.

Jake, clinging to Lisa's hand, whispered, "It looks different."

"It's the same," Lisa assured him, though her voice wavered slightly. "It just doesn't have the same power over us anymore."

Tom ran a hand along the well's weathered stone edge.

"Maybe we should fill it in," he suggested. "Make sure no one else stumbles across it."

Lisa shook her head slowly, her eyes never leaving the dark mouth of the well. "No," she said softly. "I don't think that's the answer. Some things...some forces can't be buried or forgotten. They can only be respected. And avoided."

Emily, who had been uncharacteristically quiet, spoke up. "We have to remember," she said, her young voice carrying a wisdom beyond her years. "So we can warn others."

Tom nodded, putting an arm around his daughter. "You're right, sweetheart. This is part of us now. We carry it with us so others don't have to."

The family stood in silence for a moment longer, the weight of their experience settling around them like a cloak. Then, without a word, they turned away from the well and began walking back toward their car, toward their future.

As they reached the edge of the clearing, Lisa paused and looked back. The well sat silently in the dappled light, its secrets once again hidden beneath a veil of normalcy. She took a deep breath, then turned away, following her family out of the woods and into whatever lay ahead.

As the Porters' car pulled away from Willow Creek, a palpable sense of relief mingled with an undercurrent of melancholy inside the vehicle. The family sat in contemplative silence, each lost in their own thoughts about the harrowing ordeal they'd survived and the innocence they'd left behind.

Tom's hands gripped the steering wheel tightly, his eyes fixed on the road ahead. Lisa sat beside him, occasionally glancing in the rearview mirror at their children in the backseat. Jake had dozed off, his head resting against the window, while Emily gazed out at the passing landscape, her expression unreadable.

As they passed the outskirts of town, Emily's brow

furrowed slightly. She leaned closer to the window, straining to hear something. For a brief moment, she thought she caught a whisper on the wind, faint but distinct: "Be careful what you wish for."

She shivered, pulling back from the window. "Mom?" she said softly.

Lisa turned, concern, etching her features. "What is it, sweetie?"

Emily hesitated, then shook her head. "Nothing. I just... I'm glad we're together."

Lisa reached back to squeeze her daughter's knee, a sad smile on her face. "Me too, honey. Me too."

As the car disappeared around a bend, shadows lengthened across the forest they'd left behind. Through the ancient trees, past gnarled branches, and whispering leaves, the clearing still waited. There, the old well stood, silent and seemingly innocent.

A leaf detached from a nearby branch, spiraling lazily through the air before disappearing into the well's dark depths. For a moment, all was still.

Then, in the settling silence, a soft, ominous chuckle echoed from within the well. It was barely audible, a sound that could be mistaken for the wind or imagination, yet it carried an unmistakable note of ancient malevolence.

The laughter faded, leaving behind an unsettling silence. While the Porters had escaped, closing this chapter of Malathor's story, the evil that dwelled in the well merely slumbered. It would wait, patient and eternal, for the next unwary soul to stumble upon its promise of granted wishes and terrible consequences.

The Hollow Route

ERIK
SHEIN
MELISSA
DAVIS
KAREN
FULLER

CHAPTER 1
A NIGHT LIKE ANY OTHER

THE HOLLOW ROUTE

The campus clock tower struck one, its deep resonance shattering the silence of the night. Maya Scott's head snapped up, her heart racing as the sound pulled her from her studies. How long had she been here? Her research project was consuming more than just hours; it was devouring entire nights of her life.

The library, once a sanctuary of learning, now felt alien in the early morning hours. Shadows stretched between bookshelves, transforming familiar corridors into unfamiliar terrain. Maya's gaze darted around the empty study area, suddenly aware of her solitude. Some said this floor was haunted, though she had never seen any ghosts herself. Not that she wanted to stick around to find out if some urban legend was real.

She closed her textbook with trembling hands, the soft thud echoing in the silence. As she gathered her notes, a chill ran down her spine. The quiet that had once aided her concentration now felt oppressive, watching, waiting. Her thoughts started to run away with her. Before long, she'd probably start imagining dust bunnies rallying to chase her around the library. Yes, she had been here far too long tonight. Her brain desperately needed a break from this place.

Maya slung her backpack over her shoulder, its weight

a comfort in the eerie stillness. Each step towards the exit seemed to echo louder than the last, as if the library itself was urging her to leave. Maya was happy to comply.

The air hung heavy with a silence that seemed to thicken with every moment. Even the shadows appeared to recoil from the touch of the pale moonlight streaming through the high windows, pooling in the corners like dark secrets. It was as if the library had become a mausoleum for dead thoughts, where ideas were entombed in leather-bound graves, their whispers haunting the shelves.

Maya paused, her hand on her bag's strap, the weight of unseen eyes upon her, stirring a chill that crept along her spine. The stillness was no longer merely the absence of noise but a presence, a fear laced with the premonition that she had outstayed her welcome. It was time to go before the tricks her mind played on her manifested into something real.

She shook her head, attempting to dismiss the creeping unease, attributing it to weariness. Yet, the sensation persisted, a nagging doubt that played upon her intellect, whispering that something was amiss—that the quiet was not simply eerie but unnatural. A draft, cold as the grave, stirred the air, and Maya shivered, pulling her coat tighter around her slender frame as she started her departure.

As she made her way to the exit, the rhythmic cadence of her footsteps became a staccato heartbeat in the vast, void-like expanse of the library. A place of learning by day had transformed into a gothic tableau, where the line between the real and the imagined blurred like ink on damp parchment.

"Time to go home," Maya whispered to herself, her voice a frail banner in the face of an unseen enemy. Her words hung in the air, a futile attempt to break the spell of the library's nocturnal embrace. But the echo that returned was not her own—instead, it was the library that seemed to answer, its voice a hollow reminder that some hauntings are born not of the place but of the mind.

Maya emerged from the library's oppressive silence into the night, a shroud of darkness enveloping the campus grounds. The moon struggled to break through thick, dark clouds, its pale light barely illuminating the narrow walkways. Trees stood as stoic sentinels, their twisted branches etching a black lacework against the sky.

The campus clock tower loomed overhead, its face obscured by shadows. The hands were invisible from this distance, but Maya felt them ticking away the seconds, a silent judgment on her tardiness. The grounds lay deserted, streetlights casting pools of sickly yellow light that barely penetrated the darkness between buildings.

As she approached the bus stop, the digital timetable glowed with a cold, blue light. It flickered once, twice, then steadied as the numbers declared their unwelcome news: the last bus had departed minutes ago. Maya's heart sank as the reality of her situation set in. She was alone on a campus that suddenly felt too vast, too empty.

A gust of wind rustled through nearby trees, carrying with it a whisper of something...off. Maya spun around, her eyes scanning the darkness. Nothing moved in the shadows, yet the feeling of being watched persisted.

"Get it together, Maya," she muttered, her voice small in the oppressive silence. But as she stood there, stranded and alone, Maya couldn't shake the creeping sensation that this night was about to become anything but ordinary.

The campus, with its darkened corners and whispered secrets, held her captive in its chilling embrace. Maya cast a glance over her shoulder, half-expecting to see a figure materialize from the gloom. Her breath materialized in the chill of the night as she stood, a solitary figure against the vacant canvas of the university bus stop.

With trembling fingers, Maya extracted her phone from her backpack, the screen's glow a beacon in the shadow-drenched world. She scrolled through her options, seeking an escape route from this nocturnal prison. The digital map sprawled before her eyes, yet the virtual streets offered no solace, no alternative path that would lead her safely home.

Maya's fingers danced across the screen in a ritualistic cadence, seeking the familiar comfort of predictability within the transit app. Her breath formed small puffs of mist that lingered in the cold air. The app flickered and refreshed with an unexpected message: "Bus 13 arriving in 4 minutes." No such bus existed on her usual schedule, yet there it was, manifesting as if conjured by her silent plea.

Relief washed over Maya, seeping into her bones. A brief smile dared to cross her lips, its presence as fleeting as a shadow passing over the moon. The unexpected bus was a herald of escape from this night that felt too heavy, too charged with unspoken secrets.

"Could be a glitch or a rerouted line. Looks like my lucky night," she reasoned, more to convince herself than to dispute the void. But the shadows at the edge of the deserted bus stop seemed to lean in closer, and Maya couldn't shake the feeling that her luck might be about to change.

CHAPTER 2
THE UNSCHEDULED ROUTE

THE HOLLOW ROUTE

A veil of mist descended with an unearthly grace as if the heavens themselves were exhaling a cold, phantasmal breath upon the world. Maya watched in silent awe as it twisted and curled around lampposts, swallowing the wan light in greedy gulps. It crept across the pavement, tendrils of vapor reaching out to caress her boots, shrouding the bus stop in a world removed from time.

Maya's heart raced, her senses on high alert as she stood amidst the uncanny stillness. The air seemed charged with an invisible energy, crackling and pulsing like a living entity that made the familiar surroundings feel foreign and sinister. She strained her eyes against the encroaching shadows, searching for a logical explanation but finding none. Every sound echoed strangely. Every movement seemed to leave afterimages in the air, adding to the sense of unease creeping over her skin.

Gradually, a distant rumble began to permeate the stillness, growing in volume until it echoed off the surrounding buildings. It was the raspy growl of an engine heralding the arrival of the bus that her digital oracle had promised. The sound became a symphony of revving motors and hissing brakes, filling the air with a sense of urgency and motion.

But there was something amiss in its cadence, a staccato rhythm that did not belong to the purring of well-oiled machinery. This was the clanking of chains, the grinding of gears worn by time or torment, an anthem of decay that warned of ruin and desolation.

Maya felt the ground beneath her vibrate with the impending arrival, a dull tremor that resonated with the pounding in her chest. The sound drew nearer, relentless, unforgiving—an echo of doom approaching through the impenetrable white.

And then, cutting through the fog like a blade through silk, the vehicle announced itself with a raspy roar that seemed too ancient, too fraught with hidden tales of woe, to simply be the product of combustion and steel.

"Great. When was this built, last century?" Maya had longed for a ride home, yet now, as the unseen bus pressed closer, a chill settled over her heart—a premonition of journeys that stretched beyond the mere physical into realms whispered of in hushed tones and written of in yellowed pages.

"Home..." she whispered a prayer to the night, to the fog, to whatever spirits might be listening. But the word rang hollow, a frail thing lost in the gathering storm of sounds and swirling mist.

The fog parted with an elegance that defied the natural order, revealing a bus that seemed an anomaly against the backdrop of modernity. Paint flaked from its flanks in sorrowful strips, rust spreading across its hide like a blight, while its windows—cloudy and opaque—held captive the ghosts of untold voyages.

Maya's breath caught in her throat as her mind, usually a bastion of reason and logic, roiled with disquiet. This wasn't just transportation; it was a specter on wheels, a relic that should have been buried beneath layers of time and progress. Yet here it stood before her, creaking under the weight of its own decay, offering an impossible choice: brave its mysterious passage or remain stranded in the night.

A hesitation, like a delicate flower, bloomed within Maya's chest. It took root and spread through the fertile ground of her intellect, stirring doubts and unease. Her usually rational and logical mind roiled with disquiet, unable to make sense of the mysterious vehicle before her. Its form seemed to defy all laws of probability and practicality that she held dear. It was an apparition of transportation, an otherworldly sight that both intrigued and unnerved her. She couldn't help but feel a sense of trepidation as she contemplated getting inside and embarking on this strange journey.

"What are you so afraid of? It's just a bus," she chided herself, her words a murmur lost to the encroaching fog. But her mind rebelled, conjuring images of shadowy passengers and endless, twisting roads. Her fingers twitched involuntarily as if trying to grasp reason. The air hung heavy with anticipation that tasted like copper upon the tongue — a flavor known intimately by those who stand at the threshold of the unknown, pondering whether to step across.

"An unusual one, but still..." she concluded, the scholar within clawing for a foothold against the tide of trepidation. Something about the situation gnawed at the edges of her consciousness, a dissonance in an otherwise harmonious existence. She knew the streets, the schedules, the reliable patterns of the city's veins — and this bus, this unexpected visitor, did not belong.

Yet it beckoned, an invitation whispered on the wind, a siren call woven into the very creaks and sighs of its aged frame. And Maya, despite the alarm bells pealing in the cloistered chambers of her mind, felt the pull of curiosity — the eternal plight of those devoted to knowledge, even when such pursuits skirt the periphery of peril.

Maya's limbs ached with an exhaustion that seeped into her bones, a weary testament to the long hours spent in academic pursuit. The wraithlike bus loomed before her, its presence incongruous against the canvas of reality she had painted in her mind—a world of schedules and certainties, now smeared by the brushstroke of the inexplicable.

Staring into the hollow face of this vehicular wraith, Maya wrestled with the riddles it posed. Her instincts warned her of the shadows that clung to the undercarriage, secrets as old and deep as the fog itself. But fatigue draped its leaden cloak over her shoulders, heavy with the desire for the warm embrace of home. Despite the nagging feeling of intuition, she couldn't resist the powerful urge pulling her towards it, like a mesmerizing siren's song.

The bus, as if sensing her capitulation, issued a wheeze from its rusted joints, the doors parting with a creak that sang of ancient hinges and untold stories. The sound was both an invitation and a lament to all who had crossed its threshold in times gone by. Within, the interior flickered dimly, yellowed by the feeble glow of lights that struggled to hold back the encroaching darkness.

It was within this threshold of half-light that the mysteries of the bus whispered to Maya, promising passage yet concealing its true cost. The shadows seemed to stretch forth, taloned fingers eager to caress the realm of the living. And though every sinew in her body urged caution and begged her intellect to reign supreme, the inexorable pull of necessity guided her steps towards the abyssal maw. With a heart weighed down by the stones of trepidation, Maya edged closer to the dimly lit interior, surrendering to the twin tyrants of weariness and longing.

The air itself seemed to beckon Maya, a chill whisper against her skin that murmured secrets only the night knew.

It was an inexplicable pull, a thread spun from moonlight and shadow, woven into the fabric of her exhaustion. The bus loomed like an ancient relic dredged up from forgotten depths, its entrance a gaping maw of possibilities darker than the void it promised to traverse.

Maya hesitated on the precipice of decision, her intellect warring with an unnameable urge that coiled in her gut. It was a serpent tempting her with the forbidden fruit of easy passage, hissing assurances that all would be well should she but step onto the vessel before her. Her mind swirled with questions left unanswered, with the uncanny sense that she teetered on the edge of some vast, unseen chasm, yet still, that wraithlike hand at her back nudged her forward.

"Come," the wind seemed to sigh through the fog, "come home." The words were not spoken nor heard but felt — a resonance within her marrow that spoke of shelter and solace. A clever trick of the senses, perhaps, or a deception spun by her weary desire to believe in safe harbors amidst the tempest.

With the weight of inevitability wrapped around her shoulders, Maya lifted her foot, crossing the threshold into the waiting darkness. The world outside the bus became a memory as she trod upon the worn steps, each one creaking beneath her weight as if protesting her arrival — or was it lamenting her fate?

She stood for a heartbeat in the narrow aisle, the scent of old leather and rust filling her nostrils. The interior was a tomb of half-lights and faded seats, each one like an empty coffin save for the ghosts of past passengers. They whispered to her from the shadows, their voices a tapestry of regret and longing, of journeys begun but never completed.

And then, with the inexorable finality of a closing chapter, the doors shuddered behind her, sealing Maya within the bowels of the dilapidated bus. A silence fell, heavy and absolute, as though the world held its breath, awaiting the turn of the page that would reveal the next arc of her tale.

Outside, the fog swallowed all evidence of her presence, even as the bus began its journey along the unscheduled route, towards destinations uncharted and realms whispered of only in the most fevered of nightmares. Maya, standing alone amidst the echoes of the damned, could do naught but wonder what strange ports of call awaited her in the gloom.

CHAPTER 3
WRONG TURN

THE HOLLOW ROUTE

Maya treaded softly down the aisle, her steps a hushed whisper against the subdued hum of the bus. Each passenger existed in isolated tableaux, like figures caught in amber, their forms seeming to absorb what little light remained in the space. Their presence radiated a strange gravity, cloaking Maya in a shroud of disquiet.

Her heart—a wary sentinel—kept time with the soft thrumming of the wheels against the road as she approached the driver. The driver of this unsettling procession, he towered before her, an embodiment of the grave's frigid embrace. The name Eldric was embroidered on his jacket.

"Excuse me," Maya ventured, her voice a delicate intrusion on the sepulchral quiet. She extended her hand, the coins within it clinking faintly like distant bells tolling for midnight mass.

The driver paid her no mind. His gaze was fixed on the road ahead, a road that seemed to stretch into the abyss of night itself. The stillness lingered between them, unbroken, as though her words had been swallowed by the very darkness that now seemed to press against the windows, eager to invade the dim light of the bus.

Confounded by his disregard, Maya's fingers curled around the rejected currency, her palm a cradle for the frigid metal. The coins bore the warmth of her skin for but a moment before they were returned to the sanctuary of her pocket, their brief encounter with the world at large an aborted journey.

The pallor of Eldric's skin, a canvas devoid of life's blush, remained focused on the path ahead of him, his vacant eyes reflecting nothing of her plight. He was a relic, a remnant of a bygone era where the lost wandered endlessly, searching for a destination that forever eluded their grasp. The longer she looked at him, the more his features seemed to blur. She blinked her eyes and tried to refocus her gaze on something else.

Maya retreated, sinking into the plush seat and seeking solace in its dubious comfort. The dull drone of the bus engine wove a lullaby of despair, its monotonous rhythm a harbinger of the disquiet that nestled within her bones. Her mind, trained by years of rigorous study to seek patterns and logical explanations, now recoiled from the impossible tableau unfolding around her. Every theory she'd ever learned, every rational principle she'd embraced, seemed to crumble in the face of this incomprehensible journey.

The passengers, each a reflection of abandoned hope, remained fixed in place—their vacant stares fragments of forgotten stories. In this realm of half-light and darkness, Maya sensed the thinning veil between what was known and the unfathomable depths of the unknown. Her scholarly instincts urged her to observe, to document, to understand — but how could one analyze the inexplicable?

And so, the bus trundled on, a vessel adrift in a sea of uncertainty, its course charted by a helmsman deaf to the pleas of his cargo. The fabric of reality seemed to fray at the edges, and there, in the penumbra of reason and madness, Maya sat, a solitary witness to the phantasmal journey she inadvertently boarded.

The bus lurched forward, a creak of ancient machinery that seemed to echo through the hollows of Maya's chest. An oppressive stillness descended upon the passengers, enveloping them in an invisible shroud. Not a cough nor a murmur dared to disturb the thick air, as if every breath were held captive by an unseen force.

As the cityscape unraveled beyond the murky windows, Maya noticed the route unfurling before her was one of unfamiliar turns and uncharted streets. The city she had navigated countless times during her academic career now underwent a grotesque metamorphosis. Street signs twisted into impossible shapes, their letters rearranging themselves into words that hurt her eyes to read. Familiar landmarks distorted themselves like reflections in a carnival mirror, each transformation a mockery of her memories.

The university library where she'd spent so many hours now loomed like a gothic cathedral, its windows stretching into impossible arches that seemed to pierce the very fabric of the night sky. The local café where she often studied had become a twisted parody of itself, its warm lights now casting sickly shadows that danced with malevolent purpose. Each building she passed was both familiar and alien, as if reality itself were coming undone at the seams.

Stop signs blurred past, their red octagonal faces like warning beacons she had somehow failed to heed. The streetlamps cast long, abyssal shadows that danced like wraiths alongside the moving vehicle, accomplices in this journey toward oblivion. Even the spaces between buildings seemed wrong, as if the dimensions themselves had become fluid, bending and stretching like taffy pulled by unseen hands.

A creeping sense of dislocation wrapped around Maya's mind. The roads, once etched into her memory through countless commutes, now betrayed her, twisting into patterns devoid of logic or reason. Each intersection they crossed, a silent sentry to her mounting confusion, stood as a testament to the aberrant path they traversed. Familiar street corners transformed into impossible angles, defying the very geometry she had studied in her mathematics courses.

Her intelligence, usually so sharp and so certain, faltered before this enigma, leaving her feeling untethered from the reality she knew. Years of academic training had taught her to question, to analyze, to seek rational explanations—but what explanation could there be for a world that refused to follow its own rules? The strangeness of the journey clawed at the edges of her consciousness, murmuring doubts that swirled like mist through her thoughts. The bus, a chariot of phantasms, bore her deeper into the gloom, away from the safety of the familiar.

The phantasmal bus careened forward, and Maya pressed her forehead to the cool window glass, peering out into the encroaching dusk. Buildings, once mundane in their familiarity, now towered like grotesque sentinels over the twisted streets. The campus science center, where she'd spent countless hours in the lab, rippled like a mirage in the desert heat, its modern glass façade flowing like liquid mercury. The student union building stretched impossibly tall, its roof seeming to scrape against low-hanging clouds that hadn't been there moments before. Her favorite bookstore, usually a cozy refuge of knowledge, now resembled a gothic mansion, its display windows filled with shadows that moved independently of any light source.

Façades melted into eerily elongated forms, windows blinked as if with sly, dark eyes, and doors contorted into leering mouths agape with silent laughter. Every corner she recognized became a twisted parody of itself—the neighborhood deli stretched like pulled taffy, its neon sign bleeding colors that had no names. The city she knew receded into a phantasmagoria of bending architecture and impossible geometry, a nightmare version of the streets she'd walked countless times before.

With each block they passed, the scenery grew more surreal—a macabre artist's canvas smeared by weird strokes. Brick and mortar bled into one another, the urban landscape a fever dream etched upon the world's skin. Maya's analytical mind struggled to process the impossible transformations. She had studied urban planning as part of her minor and understood the principles of architecture and city layout, but nothing in her education had prepared her for buildings that defied not just design principles but the very laws of physics themselves.

Feeling a hollow drop in her chest, Maya retrieved her phone, seeking the cold comfort of technology's guidance. But the device, too, betrayed her; its screen was void of bars, the GPS icon spinning fruitlessly in a digital gyre. The map application opened to show streets that twisted like serpents, road names that shifted and changed even as she watched. As she tapped and prodded, willing a signal to life, the truth mocked her efforts—there was no sanctuary to be found in ones and zeroes, no breadcrumb trail back to reality.

A nameless dread crept along her nerves, murmuring of distances that could not be measured in miles or minutes but in the gulf between worlds. The cellphone, now a useless talisman in her trembling grasp, seemed an absurdity amidst the solemn procession of the damned. Even the clock displayed impossible times, the digits flowing into each other like melting wax, marking the passage of moments that had no meaning in this twisted realm.

Maya clutched the lifeless phone, a relic from a world

that seemed to be slipping away with each passing moment. Her fingers twitched involuntarily against the stillness that enveloped the bus like a shroud. She rose from her seat, legs unsteady as if the ground underfoot was no longer certain. The aisle seemed to stretch and contract with each step. The physics she'd studied all her life was now nothing more than suggestions in this realm of fluid reality.

"Excuse me," her voice wavered, reaching out for contact in the void of stillness. The words fell stale and flat, devoured by the thick air. Each passenger sat like a frozen tableau, their faces obscured by darkness or turned away at unnatural angles as though they were marionettes strung up by an unseen puppeteer's caprice. She recognized in their stillness a mockery of the living world she'd left behind, each figure a silent rebuke to her desperate grasp at normalcy.

"Can anyone hear me?" she implored, a note of desperation creeping into her articulate tone. No heads turned; no eyes met hers in silent communion. They were figures carved from midnight, each one a monument to apathy. The academic part of her mind tried to catalog their appearances, to find some pattern in their arrangement, but even this analytical approach felt futile in the face of their eerie stillness.

Her mind reeled as the reality of her isolation dawned—a chilling revelation that murmured of dangers lurking just beyond perception. Maya's breath formed clouds in the stagnant atmosphere, each exhale a testament to the frigid terror that began to crystallize within her. She watched as the vapor from her breath twisted into impossible shapes before dissipating, following laws of physics that existed only in this nightmare realm.

"This isn't right," she pleaded to the indifferent audience. Her words hung lonely in the space between them, an echo of fear that found no purchase. The oppressive silence mocked her pleas, wrapping around her spirit like a winding sheet. All her years of study, all her careful observations of the natural world, crumbled before this reality that defied every law she understood. She sank back into her seat, defeated.

The bus trundled on, its journey a descent into realms unknown, and Maya stood alone amidst the congregation of the mute and the motionless — her own voice the only testimony to the living nightmare unfolding around her. Outside, the city continued its impossible dance of transformation, a visual symphony of horror that played out against the canvas of her familiar world, while inside, she remained trapped with these silent witnesses to her journey into madness.

CHAPTER 4
A FELLOW PASSENGER

THE HOLLOW ROUTE

Maya's heart hammered against her ribcage like a frantic bird seeking escape. The spectral bus, with its dim lighting and the soft hum of its engine, had become a coffin on wheels. She pressed her forehead to the cool windowpane, trying to steady her breath, but each exhalation fogged the glass and obscured the shadowy landscape beyond. It was as if the world outside retreated into the folds of oblivion, leaving Maya with the disquieting sense that she was traveling through an endless void.

A whisper, delicate as spider silk, drifted through the stale air of the bus, slicing through the fabric of Maya's panic. She stiffened, her green eyes darting in search of the source. The passengers were phantoms, their features indistinct and shrouded by the gloom, but one figure separated from the shadows with a slow, deliberate motion.

A man approached her, his form an angular silhouette against the flickering overhead lights. His face bore the etchings of someone who had journeyed through the abyss and had been remade by its harrowing touch. His hair, short and unkempt, framed a visage that spoke volumes of the spectral bus's cruel tenure.

"Listen," he murmured, his voice the echo of a distant storm. His haunted gaze locked with hers, a silent plea woven into the intensity of his stare.

Maya felt the unnerving pull of his presence, the gravity of a shared fate drawing them together within this rolling catacomb. His words hung heavily between them, a lifeline cast into the churning seas of her disbelief. Could this disheveled man, with eyes that had seen the unseeable, truly understand the nature of their plight? Or was he merely another lost soul adrift in the same dark waters as she?

The old, worn bus groaned and creaked beneath them, a reminder of the relentless passage of time. Its faded exterior and chipped paint gave it a tired, weathered appearance. Maya couldn't help but feel a sense of unease as she sat inside, the rumbling engine vibrating through her bones. The man's presence lingered in her awareness, his single word "listen" hanging in the air between them. She couldn't shake the feeling that something was about to change, the unknown looming before her like an ominous storm cloud on the horizon. The bus barreled down the highway, passing by fields and forests, a blur of green and brown out the window. Maya's heart raced as she waited for what this mysterious man might reveal.

"Shh," he hissed, his hand lifting in a swift motion to still the air between them. "Your voice—it's like a beacon here. I'm Ben," he added in a whisper, "and you are?"

"Maya," she breathed, barely audible over the engine's constant noise.

Maya's breath hitched in her throat, her lips parting slightly as she struggled to find the words to respond. Her eyes widened, trying to decipher the enigmatic tapestry of emotions woven into this stranger's urgent whisper. She was caught in a web of curiosity, fear, and excitement as she leaned closer, hoping to unravel the mystery behind this unexpected encounter.

"Understand this," Ben continued, each word measured and heavy with unspoken knowledge. "This is no chartered journey; it is a vessel ensnared in shadows. We are aboard a trap designed for souls that have lost their way."

A chill skittered down Maya's spine, coiling around her heart like a spectral serpent.

The bus was shrouded in shadows. Its windows, dark as a moonless night, mirrored nothing of the exterior abyss, serving as eerie portals into the soulless expanse beyond. Each rumble of the engine was a morbid dirge, the mournful beat of this mobile catacomb carrying the doomed on their way to oblivion. She glanced about the cabin; passengers sat too still, too silent, their faces ashen and devoid of hope.

"This vehicle," Ben murmured, his voice a low rumble of hidden depths, "gathers the wanderers, the confused... those who linger too long at life's crossroads."

Dread pooled in the hollows of Maya's stomach, the creeping horror of Ben's implications seeping into her consciousness. The bus continued to move slowly, its engine humming a mournful tune in the fading light, seemingly lamenting the destiny of its passengers.

Maya clutched the cold metal of the seat in front of her, fingers white as the spectral glow that seeped through the bus's cracked flooring. Her mind, that fortress of logic and reason, quaked under the weight of Ben's grim revelations. She had always navigated life with a compass of certainty, each step a calculated venture. But now, adrift on this endless road, the needle spun wildly, pointing to a truth she could not yet fathom.

"No way," she said, barely audible over the engine's constant noise. "Someone's definitely messing with us. This has to be some kind of prank."

Ben regarded her with eyes that had witnessed

countless denials crumble into acceptance. Those haunted orbs held a glimmer of compassion for her disbelief, even as his words carved the air with stark clarity.

"Look around you, Maya," he said, his tone hushed but insistent. "Feel the life being siphoned from your very marrow. This bus is not bound by earthly roads; it roams the boundaries of existence, a purgatory on wheels."

She recoiled from the notion, her intellect clawing for a rational explanation. Yet beneath the veneer of skepticism, a primal instinct twisted inside her—a serpent of doubt shedding its skin of normalcy.

"Life force?" The question emerged from her lips before she could tether it, giving voice to the growing unease that gnawed at her sanity.

"Indeed," Ben murmured, leaning closer so the others might not overhear. "A roving parasite that feeds on the essence of the ensnared, cloaked in the mundane guise of transportation. It drains us slowly, so we do not notice until it's too late—until we become nothing more than husks, faded echoes of our former selves."

"Then why are you still here?" she asked, the question a lifeline thrown into the abyss of her mind.

"Because I've learned how to resist, how to keep my spirit anchored despite the pull of oblivion." Ben's voice had taken on the cadence of a confession, the rhythm of a heart fighting against the encroaching darkness.

"Resist?" Maya echoed, her skepticism a frail shield against the onslaught of possibilities that loomed before her.

"Trust me," he implored, his gaze never leaving hers. "I can guide us out of this nocturnal reverie, but only if you believe."

The engine droned on, a requiem for the lost as the bus continued its odyssey through the twilight. And Maya, caught between the tangible world she knew and the phantasmal realm that beckoned, felt the first tendrils of dread snake their way into her resolve.

The bus groaned under the weight of shadows that seemed to cling to its frame, a hungry beast devouring the distance with an insatiable appetite. Maya's breath came in short bursts, her gaze darting from window to window, searching for some sign of familiarity in the murky landscape beyond.

"Look," Ben murmured, his finger trembling as it pointed towards the floor. "See how the shadows are deeper than they should be, even for this time of night?"

Maya followed his gesture and noted the darkness pooling beneath the seats, an abyssal black that drank in the meager light. It was as though the shadows were alive, whispering secrets as they danced just out of reach. The sight sent a shiver coursing down her spine, a visceral response to a threat that was more felt than seen.

"And there—" Ben's voice wavered as he indicated the windows, "the reflections are wrong, distorted as if we're looking into a world that doesn't quite belong to us."

Maya peered closer, her eyes narrowing. Indeed, the glass seemed to warp their images, twisting them into grotesque caricatures. Her own reflection bore little resemblance to the face she knew; her features elongated and eyes hollow, it gazed back with an accusatory stare that spoke of guilt and hidden fears.

"Can't you feel it, Maya?" Ben's question pierced the veil of her disbelief, a needle drawing blood from the heart of her skepticism. "The way the air is thick, almost suffocating? It's the life being leeched from us, second by second."

She could deny it no longer — the heaviness that draped over her shoulders like a funeral shroud, the lethargy that sought to chain her limbs and spirit. It was subtle, yes, but undeniably present, a malevolent force that toyed with her senses and mocked her reason.

"Perhaps it's just our imagination," Maya offered weakly, clinging to the remnants of logic like a drowning sailor to a splintered mast.

"Is it?" Ben's eyes held a challenge, a dare to confront the reality of their grim theatre. "Or have we simply been blind to the truth that lurks behind the veil of what we deem possible?"

The words hung in the air, spectral and condemning. Maya wrestled with her thoughts, each breath a battle between the empirical truths she had always embraced and the strange evidence that now demanded recognition. The comfort of denial crumbled, leaving her exposed to the creeping horror that slithered through the crevices of her mind.

Outside, the world passed by in a blur of shapes and shadows, indifferent to the plight of the souls ensnared within the roving purgatory. Inside, Maya stood at the precipice of understanding, the ground beneath her feet crumbling as she teetered between the realms of the living and the damned.

The bus shuddered as if in the throes of a dark incantation, its wheels grinding against the unseen cogs of fate. Maya's thoughts spun with it, a carousel of dread and disbelief. She clutched the seat before her, knuckles blanching, as the dim light flickered overhead like the dying pulse of a spectral heart.

"Listen to me," Ben murmured, his voice a hoarse whisper that cut through the suffocating silence. "There's a crossroads coming up. It's our only shot."

Maya's breath caught, a fragile hope amidst the encroaching shadows. The crossroads—a concept so mundane, yet now it whispered secrets of liberation. Her mind reeled, grasping at the edges of this newfound revelation.

"Crossroads?" she echoed, the words tasting of ancient rites and forbidden thresholds.

"Exactly," he said, nodding with a fervor that belied his weariness. "A place of power, liminality. Where worlds collide and the rules that bind us...fray."

The bus lurched again, a mocking nod to the gravity of their conversation. Outside, the night was a relentless abyss, the road a serpent slithering into the unknown.

"The crossroads exist in the cracks of reality, a place where one can break free from their entanglements," continued Ben.

"Can we trust it? This escape you speak of?" Maya's voice trembled, not from fear alone but from the weight of decision that now rested upon her slender shoulders. The academic within her clamored for evidence, for data, and peer-reviewed research. But here, in the belly of this beast, the empirical truths seemed like phantoms, insubstantial and mocking.

"You don't have to trust me," Ben replied, his eyes pools of sincerity floating in a sea of torment. "But trust your instincts. Those same instincts that are screaming at you that nothing about this place is right."

Maya peered into the void beyond the grimy window, searching for the fabled crossroads as if willing it to pierce the darkness and beckon them forth. Her intellect warred with her primal, human yearning for salvation, each argument a stroke upon the canvas of her unraveling sanctuary of logic.

"Time is slipping," Ben pressed, urgency lacing his tone. "We need to be ready to act when the moment comes."

The bus, a chariot of sorrow, bore them towards the unseen juncture with indifferent momentum. Maya closed her eyes, inhaling the stale, charged air. When she opened them again, her green irises glinted, not with certainty, but with the resolve of a woman who knew that to remain motionless was to succumb to the abyss.

"Tell me what I need to do," she whispered, and the words were a covenant sealed with the currency of the damned — their very souls teetering on the knife edge between perdition and possibility.

CHAPTER 5
TERRIBLE TRUTHS

THE HOLLOW ROUTE

The spectral bus groaned as it took another tight turn, its metal frame screeching against the invisible forces that guided it along a desolate and never-ending road. Ben sat hunched over, his gaunt form a shadow among shadows, his fingers knotted together as if in prayer or pain—it was hard to discern which.

"Months," he said, the word falling from his lips like a stone into still water. "I've been here for months."

He did not look at the one he spoke to; instead, his haunted gaze seemed to pierce through the grimy window, seeking something beyond. His voice, weary yet earnest, carried the weight of untold stories, each syllable saturated with the essence of his captivity.

"Time is a trickster here. Days, nights—they bleed together, an endless loop of despair." Ben's eyes flickered momentarily towards her, acknowledging the shared nightmare. "But there are rules to this prison. Rules I've learned at great cost."

"Rules?" Her voice was a whisper, barely rising above the eerie silence that had settled like a shroud over the bus's occupants.

"Ah, yes," he nodded slowly, his unkempt beard bristling with the motion. "The first is that time doesn't pass—

not as we know it. The second, we can't force our egress. It's not about where the bus goes, but rather when it decides to release you — if ever."

His words hung heavy in the air, a chilling testament to a reality that defied understanding. His eyes, deep wells of sorrow, now held a spark of defiance.

"Another thing," Ben continued, the rhythm of his speech matching the intermittent flicker of the dim overhead lights, "is that intent matters here. Wishing to leave isn't enough. One must understand the nature of this place to navigate its deceit."

"Deceit?" she echoed, her own breath catching on the edge of a new, uncomfortable truth.

"Every shadow here whispers lies. Every reflection hides a secret." He leaned closer, and for a moment, she could see the fire that burned within him, the unyielding spirit that refused to be extinguished. "You must listen but never trust. Observe, but do not believe. The walls have ears and the windows eyes. And all of it, every inch, is eager to ensnare us further."

As the bus continued its relentless journey through the murky landscape, the atmosphere grew thick with unsaid words and buried fears. In the gloom, Ben's presence was a beacon — a guide through the darkness, even as he himself was consumed by it.

"Escape is a delicate art," he murmured, and the bus seemed to resent the notion, its engine emitting a low, ominous growl. "But it's possible. I've seen it — almost tasted freedom once. There's a pattern to discern, a riddle to solve."

"Tell me," her voice was steadier now, demanding, desperate for the sliver of hope he offered.

"Patience," Ben cautioned, his eyes narrowing slightly as if remembering a painful lesson. "We will speak more. For now, watch, listen, learn. The crossroads approach, and with them, a chance."

A silent pact formed in the gloom, a fragile alliance between two souls adrift in this eerie limbo. And as the bus trundled on, the night itself seemed to hold its breath, awaiting the next move in a game as old as sin.

A cold shiver crept down Maya's spine; the air around her felt unusually dense, and the bus's wheels thudded against the uneven road like a slow, methodical heartbeat. She clutched the frayed edge of the seat, knuckles whitening, as she stared into Ben's haunted eyes. His tale of entrapment—a chronicle of months swallowed by an abyss—echoed in her mind, refusing to settle into the realm of credibility.

"Months?" Her voice was a fragile whisper, grappling with the edges of Ben's dark narrative. "But that's impossible. I have exams, a graduation... My family..." The words splintered as they left her lips, the life she knew fracturing before the relentless march of this grim reality.

"Time," Ben said with a hollow chuckle, "is one of their crueler jests here." He gestured vaguely toward the murky windows where shadows seemed to swim against the glass. "It bends and stretches, warping until you forget the taste of yesterday or the color of tomorrow."

Maya's eyes darted to the other passengers, searching for some sign of humanity, a flicker of warmth. But each face was a blurred echo of existence, their features indistinct and smeared, like charcoal drawings smudged by careless fingers. They sat motionless, silent guardians of a secret too terrible to voice.

"Look at them," Ben whispered, his tone laced with a heavy sorrow. "They were once like us, full of hope and fire. Now they're nothing but wraiths, hollow shells lost to despair."

Her breath hitched as realization dawned with chilling clarity. These were not fellow wayfarers on a late-night route; they were remnants of souls, forsaken and forgotten. The knowledge settled upon her like a shroud, the spectral bus an eternal ferryman on Stygian waters.

"Are we to become like them?" The question emerged from a place of primal fear. The academic rigor that once fortified her reduced to mere whispers against this occult tempest.

"Only if we let it consume us," he replied, his voice a beacon against the creeping tide of dread. "Remember who you are, Maya Scott. Your will is your own. Cling to it."

The bus groaned under the weight of their defiance, its interior dimming as though night itself was infiltrating its confines, suffusing the air with a palpable malevolence. Maya's heart drummed a frantic rhythm, yet within that terror, a defiant spark kindled. Her resolve hardened—she would not yield so easily to this phantasmal trap.

"Then we fight," she stated, her voice gaining strength from the embers of her determination. "We find our way back."

"Indeed," Ben agreed, a ghost of a smile tugging at his weary features. "At the crossroads, we make our stand."

The bus continued its inexorable journey through the darkness, the road ahead uncertain, while inside, two souls braced against the encroaching shadows, their plight woven into the fabric of this nocturnal tapestry. And beyond the thin veil of reality, the night whispered of secrets and sins, the past reaching out with tendrils of remorse to ensnare the unwary.

Ben's voice was a low thrum that seemed to blend with the shadows that clung to the corners of their prison on wheels."Once, a man thought sheer force would free us. He charged the doors at every stop. They never opened for him.

After the third try, he simply...unraveled. Became like the others — less than wraiths, mere echoes."

Maya's breath caught in her throat, the chilling image searing into her mind. "And no one has ever just...left? At a stop?"

"Left?" The word hung between them, mocking in its simplicity. "Yes, they've left the bus, stepped out into the world beyond — but it's not our world, Maya. It's a cruel mimicry, a trap baited with false hope."

"Then what is this place?" she asked, her green eyes wide as they sought his in the gloom, searching for an anchor in the maelstrom of madness. "Where are we, really?"

"Limbo or purgatory, perhaps," Ben mused, gazing out the window at the darkness that seemed almost viscous in its opacity. "A place for souls lost, not yet knowing they're damned."

"Damned?" Maya echoed, the word tasting bitter on her tongue, an affront to her senses. "But why? What have we done to deserve this?"

"Who can say?" His shoulders shrugged, a weary gesture beneath the weight of countless unanswered questions. "Perhaps it's not about what we've done, but what we failed to do."

"Failed..." Her voice faltered, the academic rigor that had always been her compass now failing to chart a course through this supernatural quagmire. She pressed on, driven by the need to understand, to dissect this enigma. "Is there no pattern, no common thread among those who've tried to leave?"

"None that reveals itself plainly," he replied, his face half-hidden in shadow, giving him the aspect of a half-remembered dream. "Some fought, some acquiesced. All remained."

"Remained," she repeated, a shiver coursing through her despite the still air. "As though the bus feeds on our despair..."

"Feeds, yes," Ben agreed, his gaze distant, as if peering into realms denied to the living. "Or perhaps it merely wishes to keep its collection intact. We are curiosities, specimens pinned to velvet in a display case."

"Specimens..." Maya murmured. Her scientific mind rebelled against the notion, even as the evidence of her senses corroborated the grim hypothesis. "Then, how do we break the cycle?"

"By understanding the rules," Ben said, turning to her with an intensity that belied his fatigue. "By finding the flaw in the design."

"Rules and flaws..." Maya's thoughts raced, her determination reigniting amidst the darkness. There had to be a way to unravel the tapestry of this nightmare, to find the loose thread and pull.

"Tell me," she implored, her voice steadier now, a reflection of the resolve hardening within her. "Everything you know."

Ben nodded, and as the bus trundled further into the night, its every creak and groan a whispered threat, he began to recount tales of past attempts, of strategies employed and dangers braved — all fallen short of freedom's threshold. And as he spoke, Maya listened, her mind alight with the fire of inquiry, already probing the edges of their eerie puzzle for weaknesses to exploit.

"Listen to me, Maya," he said, the weight of his gaze pinning her with an urgency that made her spine stiffen. "This isn't just a prison of steel and sorrow; it's one of the mind, too. The moment you let doubt gnaw at your resolve, you've already lost."

Maya clenched her fists, knuckles white as the ghostly pallor outside. She understood now—the bus feasted on weakness and thrived on the uncertainty that crept like ivy through the cracks of one's will.

"Then what?" she asked, the words etched with a newfound fortitude. "What do we cling to?"

"Belief," he stated simply, yet the word echoed with the profundity of ancient incantations. "You have to believe in something stronger than the fear it conjures."

"Belief," she repeated, tasting the concept, rolling it around in her thoughts until it took root. It was not the sterile belief of data and observable facts she was accustomed to but a primal kind born of desperation and the raw human spirit.

"Exactly." Ben's nod was almost imperceptible in the gloom. "And there's more. We can't fight the nature of this place, but perhaps we can use it. Bend its rules to our favor."

"Go on," Maya urged, her curiosity a beacon amidst the encroaching darkness.

"Every time this cursed vehicle crosses the crossroads, there's a flicker, a stutter in the air. A glitch in the matrix of this hell," Ben whispered, leaning closer as if sharing a sacred secret. "It's then that the veil between here and the real world thins—a sliver of dawn in eternal night."

"Is that when we make our move?" Her voice held a tremble, not of fear but of anticipation.

"It has to be." He drew back, eyes scanning the dim interior, wary of unseen listeners. "When we approach the crossroads again, we'll need to focus all our intent, every fiber of our being, on where we want to emerge. Doubt is the enemy; it will scatter our efforts like leaves in a gale."

"Intent," she mused, the concept settling in her chest, a small flame against the cold.

"More than intention—a fierce, unyielding demand of

the universe to set things right." Ben's demeanor suggested a man who had walked through infernos and emerged scorched but unbowed.

"Have you tried…"

"Once," he cut her off, and she saw the memory flicker behind those haunted eyes—a tempest contained. "I wasn't ready then. But together, with a shared purpose, we might stand a chance."

"Then we prepare," Maya decided, her voice steadier than she felt, each syllable a stone laid on the path out of perdition. "We'll bring something this bus has never seen before."

"Indeed." Ben nodded, his approval palpable as the darkness seemed to lean in, curious and cautious. "We'll turn their trap into our doorway."

A silence settled over them, punctuated only by the relentless hum of the engine. In that hush, they were not merely passengers but conspirators etching a plan onto the fabric of their eerie reality. They would stand at the crossroads, armed with nothing but will and belief, and dare to defy the malevolent forces that sought to bind them to this endless purgatory.

The rhythmic thrum of the bus engine, once a monotone lullaby, had transformed into the pulse of an unseen predator. Maya felt it resonate through her bones—a harbinger of their daring defiance against this spectral prison. In the thickening gloom, her heart became a metronome for her burgeoning resolve.

"Ben," she whispered, her voice threading through the oppressive silence, "we cannot let fear dictate our fate."

The air within the bus grew dense as though the shadows themselves were weaving a tapestry of dread around them. It was a subtle shift, unnoticed by the wraith-like passengers, but Maya sensed it with a clarity that sharpened her focus. The windows, which should have offered a view of the outside world, now held only reflections of despair.

"Indeed," Ben replied, his tone bearing the weight of countless lost hours. His eyes, reflecting the dim light, flickered with the same determination that now fueled Maya's spirit.

The bus turned a corner, its wheels grinding against the road as if reluctant to follow its own predetermined path. The sound grated against Maya's nerves, a reminder of the stakes at hand. She leaned forward, her slender fingers entwined tightly in her lap, a knot of anticipation.

"Are we mere puppets then, dancing on the strings of this haunted stage?" Maya mused aloud, her words painting her audacity in the face of their grim reality. It was not a question seeking an answer but a declaration of rebellion.

As the bus continued its ceaseless journey, the atmosphere thickened further, adopting a palpable hostility. It seemed to press against Maya's skin, a smothering shroud attempting to quell the fire of her newfound tenacity. Each breath became a silent battle, inhaling fortitude, exhaling the remnants of trepidation.

"Remember," Ben cautioned, his voice a low murmur that barely cut through the growing malaise, "the true nature of our enemy is not of flesh and blood but of something far more insidious."

Maya nodded, her gaze unwavering. She understood that the real adversary was not the bus itself but the force that animated its cursed existence. Past sins and regrets lurked in every corner, whispering tales of despair, hoping to seduce them back into complacency.

Yet, in this moment, Maya's past transgressions did not haunt her; they steeled her. She had spent a lifetime chasing knowledge, understanding the world around her through the lens of logic. Now, she was called upon to believe in the unbelievable, to fight a foe beyond the scope of reason.

"We'll break free," she declared, her voice a resonant challenge to the creeping horror that enveloped them. Her eyes blazed with a fierce intensity, reflecting not just the somber light but also the fiery essence of her soul.

The bus seemed to respond, its ambiance turning ever more sinister, the temperature dropping like a stone in water. The other passengers, those wretched wraiths, stirred restlessly, sensing the tectonic shift in their midst. An unspoken threat hung in the air, as heavy as the darkness that sought to suffocate hope.

And though the very fibers of the bus fought against them, clawing at the edges of their plot, Maya's determination only solidified. There was no turning back. The crossroads awaited, and with them, either salvation or eternal damnation. But she would not falter—not when freedom beckoned with such a relentless call.

CHAPTER 6
GATHERING COURAGE

THE HOLLOW ROUTE

A shiver crept up Maya's spine as she ran her gaze over the bus's interior, an oppressive silence settling around them like a thick fog. The once benign patterns on the fabric of the seats now seemed to writhe subtly under her scrutiny, whispering secrets only madness could decipher. Even the air felt heavier, carrying a scent of decay that had not been there before, confirming Ben's claims in silent testimony.

"Can you see it?" Ben's voice was rough, almost lost beneath the hum of the engine like a forgotten prayer, yet it sliced through the stillness with grave urgency.

Maya nodded, her eyes reluctant to tear away from the shifting shadows that played across the walls. "It's like the bus is...alive."

"More than you know," he replied, his haunted gaze following her every movement.

The passengers, mere peripherals in her previous regard, began to stir, no longer the weary travelers she might have ignored any other day. A woman four seats ahead twisted her neck at an unnatural angle, her eyes glowing with an eerie luminescence as they locked onto Maya's. Another, a man with gaunt features, cracked his jaw open impossibly wide, emitting a low, guttural sound that scraped against Maya's nerves like claws on chalk.

"Focus on me, Maya." Ben's command was a lifeline tossed into the whirlpool of fear threatening to drag her under. His presence was a beacon amid the encroaching darkness, and she clung to it desperately. "Don't let them see your fear."

She tried to obey, but the transformation unraveled her composure. Limbs elongated, skin paled to translucence, and whispers filled the air, each passenger revealing their true, inhuman nature. It was as if the veil had been lifted, and the grotesque pantomime that played out before her was a scene plucked from the deepest pit of a nightmare.

"Ben, what are they?" Her voice trembled despite her best efforts to steady it, the words barely escaping her tight throat.

"Shadows of what they once were — or perhaps never were at all." His eyes never left hers, a silent promise that he would not let her face this horror alone. "They're part of the bus, part of the trap that's meant to drain us, to feed on our essence."

A rictus grin spread across the face of the nearest passenger, a mockery of human expression that sent a chill straight to Maya's bone marrow. The figure extended a hand with fingers too long, too jointed, reaching for her with an insatiable hunger written in its movements.

"Resist it, Maya," Ben murmured, gripping her arm with a strength that belied his worn appearance. "Remember who you are. Remember why we must escape."

As the bus trundled onward into the abyssal night, Maya, whose mind had always been her greatest ally, now found herself in a battle for her very soul against the creeping horror that sought to claim them both.

The spectral bus moved relentlessly forward, a spectral predator consuming the abandoned road beneath ghostly wheels. Maya's piercing green eyes were fixed on Eldric, the driver, searching desperately for any flicker of mortality within him. But the man maneuvered with the mechanical stiffness of a wind-up toy. His movements were devoid of the fluid sway that characterized life's dance; each action was an eerie parody of vitality's ballet. When he swiveled his head in response to murmurs from his ghostly charges, his gaze bore no glimmer of a soul but were merely vacant beacons in the gloomy shelter of the bus. His presence was a chilling reminder that they were traversing territories beyond mortal comprehension and control, his every gesture echoing with an unsettling mantra: This is not a place for the living.

"Focus on my voice," Ben's directive sliced through the encroaching terror, pulling Maya back from the brink of panic. "Your mind is a fortress. It can withstand more than you know."

She turned to him, his face etched with the grim determination of a man who had been sculpted by adversity. He was right. She could not let fear consume her. She had to be as resilient as the books that lined the shelves of her sanctuary, each spine straight and unyielding.

"Visualize a barrier," he continued, his words paced like a metronome in the chaos, "around your thoughts, around your essence. See it as a shield, repelling their intrusion."

Maya closed her eyes. In her mind's eye, she erected walls of stern stone around her, fortified with the iron will of her intellect. The whispers of the contorted passengers crashed against her defenses in vain, their insidious tendrils recoiling from her newfound strength.

"Good, Maya," Ben whispered, his voice a low hum of approval. "Hold onto that image. Let it ground you."

The world outside the windows warped further into a tapestry of nightmares—a landscape bereft of stars, where shadows writhed beneath a moonless sky. But in the cocoon of Ben's instructions, Maya found a sliver of solace. As long as she clung to her mind, to the reality she knew, she could resist being pulled into the abyss that sought to claim her soul.

"Remember, we are not like them," Ben said, his gaze steady upon her. "We are not lost yet."

In the strange interplay of light and shadow, Maya sensed the weight of his past, the regrets that haunted him. But in that shared gaze, there was also a silent vow — a promise that they would not become another twisted echo within the bus's confines.

"Keep that shield up, Maya," he urged, the rhythm of his voice both a warning and a comfort. "We're going to need every ounce of your resolve when we reach the crossroads."

Amidst the dim glow of the bus's flickering overhead lights, Maya's slender fingers traced a pattern in the air, mimicking Ben's precise movements. They were weaving invisible threads of resistance, gestures that carried the weight of their will against the unseen forces that hungered for their spirits. The dance of their hands was silent but potent, each motion a spell of defiance.

"Focus on the center of your being," Ben instructed, his voice a low murmur that seemed to harmonize with the thrumming engine. "Picture it as an unyielding fortress, impervious to the corruption around us."

Maya closed her eyes, envisioning a citadel within her mind, its ramparts imbued with the essence of her determination. She could feel the architecture of her thoughts solidifying, the stones of resolve interlocking to form an impenetrable sanctuary.

"Good, good," Ben nodded, though his brows were furrowed with the knowledge of battles lost and won. "Let that fortress be your anchor as we sever ourselves from this place."

With each repetition of the technique, Maya's confidence swelled like a tide. Her breaths became steady, and within her chest, a spark of rebellion ignited, fanned by the winds of their shared purpose.

As they practiced, the bus groaned beneath them, its chassis an echo chamber for the souls it had ensnared. Maya felt the vehicle's sinister pulse, and her awareness broadened, stretching beyond the superficial reality she had known.

The very fabric of the bus revealed itself to her—a tapestry woven with darkness and sorrow. The seats, once innocuous fixtures, now appeared as pews in a cathedral of despair, hosting congregations of grotesque shadows that whispered secrets not meant for the living. The windows, no longer mere glass, shimmered with the reflections of lives consumed, specters trapped in a never-ending journey to oblivion.

Each passenger, their features growing ever more distorted, murmured in tongues that twisted the air. They were marionettes animated by the malignant will of the bus, their strings pulled by a puppeteer that reveled in the macabre performance.

"Can you see it now?" Ben asked, his voice a thread of sanity in the enveloping madness.

Maya nodded, a shiver coursing through her frame. "It's as if the veil has been lifted, and all I see is malevolence masquerading as reality."

"Stay strong," he said, his hand finding hers in a grasp that was both comforting and anchoring. "Our vision is clear, our will steadfast. We cannot let go now."

Together, they fortified their minds against the onslaught of horror that sought to erode their humanity. The bus, sensing their burgeoning power, rumbled with displeasure. But Maya and Ben held firm, their resolve a lighthouse amidst the storm, guiding them toward the hope of escape.

As the crossroads loomed closer, the sense of impending climax swelled within the claustrophobic confines of the bus, and with it, the certainty that their confrontation with the ethereal force that steered their fate was inevitable.

The bus trundled along, its wheels drumming a dirge upon the pitted road. Maya peered through the grimy window beside her, the glass cold and unwelcoming to her touch. The landscape outside betrayed the laws of nature, contorting with each passing moment into an ever more grotesque tableau. Trees bled their colors into the sky, painting it with a palette of nightmares while shadows danced with glee at the edges of her vision.

"Ben," Maya's voice was a mere whisper, as if afraid to disturb the phantasmal scene unfolding before them. "Look."

He followed her gaze, his eyes scanning the twisted vista. "It's changing," he said, the solemnity in his tone mirroring the gravity of their plight. "We're not just moving through space, but through madness itself."

The air hung heavy with a sense of foreboding, as though reality were but a thin veil, behind which lurked entities that mocked the very essence of existence. The world outside no longer resembled anything familiar; it was a fever dream given form, a place where the subconscious fears of humanity were given reign.

In this desolate domain, Ben and Maya found solace in each other's presence. His hand still clasped hers with an earnestness that anchored her to what remained of their shared reality. She drew on his strength, feeling the courage that radiated from his touch infiltrate her being, steeling her against the encroaching terror.

"Remember what we practiced," Ben said, his words a

mantra against the dark. "Focus your mind. Don't let it feed on your fear."

Maya nodded, closing her eyes to shut out the ghastly spectacle. In the darkness behind her lids, she sought the inner sanctum of her will, a fortress built from their combined resolve. The bus seemed to sense their defiance, and the atmosphere within grew denser, a tangible pressure that sought to crush their spirits.

"Stay with me," Ben urged, his voice a beacon in the tumultuous sea of her mind. "We are the masters of our fate, not this...abomination."

The rhythm of her heart became a drumbeat, syncing with Ben's, a harmonious resistance against the discordant melody played by the bus. Their breaths mingled, a shared cadence that spoke of unity and determination. The bus groaned, its spectral passengers stirring restlessly, sensing the burgeoning power of two souls intertwined against the dark.

"Whatever happens," Maya said, opening her eyes to meet Ben's haunted gaze, "we face it together."

"We can do this," he replied, his words a vow that cut through the gloom like the first light of dawn piercing the night.

Outside, the nightmarish landscape recoiled as if repelled by the purity of their joined wills. The trees ceased their macabre dance, the sky paused in its morbid metamorphosis, and for a fleeting moment, the world held its breath.

In the eerie stillness, Maya and Ben fortified their hearts, drawing upon a wellspring of collective courage that defied the oppressive weight of the unnatural realm. They were but two souls, yet within them burned a fire that could illuminate even the darkest corners of this alien world.

The spectral bus wound its way toward the heart of desolation. Maya's eyes, luminous with resolve, scanned the interior as it morphed subtly, the eerie shapes and shadows playing tricks on her weary mind. Beside her, Ben's fingers drummed against his knee—a steady, rhythmic pulse that betrayed the urgency of their plan.

"Crossroads ahead," he murmured, words barely audible over the hum of the engine. "We jump when the two roads meet—the liminal space might weaken the veil."

Maya nodded, her thoughts whirring like cogs in a clockwork of escape. She envisioned the crossroads, a place where reality could fracture, where they might slip through the crevices of this nightmarish existence. Yet the bus seemed to anticipate their intentions, groaning with a sentient awareness that sent shivers down her spine.

"Focus," Ben said, touching her arm, grounding her. "Remember the anchors we spoke of—think of your family, your hopes. Let them be your shield."

She closed her eyes, summoning images of her loved ones, of sunlit afternoons spent in the quiet embrace of the library. These memories wrapped around her psyche, fortifying her will against the draining effect of the bus. They were more than mere thoughts; they were the essence of her being, an indomitable force that no paranormal entity could extinguish.

"Good," Ben affirmed, sensing her renewed strength. "When the moment comes, we move without hesitation."

"Without fear," Maya added, her voice a whisper of silk and steel.

As the crossroads approached in the vast distance, reality itself began to unravel, the fabric of existence tearing at the seams. Visions flickered at the corners of Maya's vision—specters of what was and what might never be, each more unsettling than the last. The world outside twisted into grotesque forms, landscapes contorted by unseen hands, skies painted with the colors of nightmares.

Maya anchored herself to Ben's presence, to the certainty that they were more than pawns in this macabre game. Their hands clasped, a lifeline amidst the chaos, their joined grip a testament to the human spirit that clawed for freedom.

CHAPTER 7
THE NATURE OF THE BEAST

THE HOLLOW ROUTE

Maya felt the world close in, a shroud of despair as she huddled with Ben. Their breaths mingled, a fog of uncertainty between them. "Remember," Ben's voice was a whisper, a ghost of sound in the oppressive silence. "Keep your gaze fixed. Don't let them see fear."

She nodded, her eyes scanning the cramped space of the spectral bus. Each passenger, once human in the dim light of memory, now seemed a grotesque parody of their former selves. Skin stretched over too-sharp bones, and eyes—too luminous, too knowing—watched the world with an alien detachment. Maya fought the urge to recoil. Instead, she studied them with the cold precision of an academic dissecting a peculiar specimen.

"Keep your mind clear," Ben cautioned, his eyes reflecting the haunted knowledge of months trapped within this liminal purgatory. "They feed off confusion, thrive on it."

"Clear...yes," Maya echoed, though her voice faltered. She had been taught to question the world, not to fear it. But these were no mere subjects for debate or analysis; they were horrors made flesh. Her intelligence, that beacon which had always illuminated the path forward, now flickered in the gathering gloom of their intentions.

Spines curled into unnatural arches, fingers lengthened

into claws beneath the flicker of sickly lights. Their presence was a stain upon reality, an abomination mocking the laws of nature. Maya felt a chill that seeped into her bones, a harbinger of dread. She clung to her determination like a shield, but even steel can yield under relentless pressure.

"Focus on the plan," Ben's voice anchored her adrift thoughts. His presence was a bulwark against the tide of monstrosities. He spoke of escape, each word etched with the gravity of one who knew the cost of failure all too well.

She tried to mirror his resolve, but her heart beat a frantic rhythm, betraying her veneer of calm. The other passengers, the entities that shared this cursed journey, they were watching. Always watching. It was as if they knew her every thought, every shiver of doubt.

"Close now," Ben breathed, his gaunt figure tense with anticipation. "We're almost at the crossroads."

Maya swallowed hard, the thickness in the air congealing around her throat like hands grasping at her will to survive. Still, she leaned closer to Ben, their whispered strategy a lifeline amidst the encroaching darkness.

As the bus trundled onward, a requiem for hope, the inhuman passengers continued their silent vigil. And Maya, with her verdant eyes that had once seen only the promise of knowledge, now stared into the abyss, where not just her life but her very soul hung in the balance.

The bus lumbered through the night, its metal bones creaking with sinister intent. Maya could feel it — the very fabric of the vehicle was no longer indifferent steel and glass but a living entity with a pulse of malice thrumming through its veins. The windows vibrated ever so slightly, not in tune with the rough asphalt beneath them, but to some otherworldly heartbeat that sought to synchronize with her own.

She pressed her palm against the seat, expecting the cold resistance of synthetic leather, but recoiled at the sensation of it breathing beneath her touch. It expanded and contracted, organic and alien, like the chest cavity of some slumbering beast. The air reeked of ozone and decay, an electric stench that heralded storms yet unseen.

"Maya," Ben's voice was a low murmur, barely rising above the whisper of the bus's malevolent life force. She turned to him, her eyes wide with unspoken fears, seeking solace in his steady gaze.

But as she looked around, the interior of the bus contorted before her eyes—a funhouse mirror reflection of reality twisted by a deranged artist's hand. Corners where there should be none, angles that defied Euclidean logic, and spaces that stretched into infinity only to collapse back upon themselves in the blink of an eye. It was a geometry of madness, a place where the laws of physics came to die.

Maya's mind reeled at the impossibility of it all, her academic brilliance grappling with the raw chaos that unfolded around her. Her studies and her pursuit of knowledge had always been her anchor, her compass. But here, what use were theorems and hypotheses when faced with the grotesque architecture of the abyss?

Beneath the stoic surface of her green-eyed resolve, something primal screamed for release. Not the scream of one who confronts terror head-on but the silent howl of a soul witnessing the unraveling of everything it once understood. Panic clawed at the edges of her composure, beckoning her to glance into the void and let madness consume her.

Yet, Maya held fast. She channeled her fear into focus, her doubt into defiance. With each breath that felt like inhaling shards of the void, she fortified the ramparts of her mind. There was no turning back—not when the crossroads loomed near, not when escape was a mere heartbeat away from the clutches of this sentient prison on wheels.

The bus groaned, a sound that might have been mistaken for the settling of age if not for the intention behind it, a growling threat to any who dared defy its dominion. And amidst the shadows that danced just beyond perception, Maya sat, a study in courage wrought from the darkest of trials.

"Listen closely," Ben whispered, the urgency in his voice a stark contrast to the oppressive stillness of the bus. His eyes, twin pools reflecting years of torment, locked with Maya's. "When the crossroads come into clear view, we jump. Whatever you see, whatever you hear, do not hesitate."

Maya nodded, her senses sharpening at the mention of their impending leap from the spectral trap that ensnared them. She noted the tremble in Ben's gaunt hand as he pointed toward the hazy outline of the promised nexus beyond the grimy window. "Ignore the forms that slip through the corners of your eyes," Ben continued, "they are but distractions, conjured by this beast to sway you."

The bus shuddered as if provoked by the conspiracy unfurling within its bowels. A low hum began to resonate through the floorboards, creeping up their spines, an unholy vibration seeking to disrupt their very marrow. It resonated with an intelligence that was neither benign nor indifferent; it was an ancient cunning, a predator cloaked in the guise of transportation.

"Remember, the entity feeds on hesitation," Ben intoned, his voice a lifeline amidst the rising cacophony of whispers and wails that seemed to seep from the vehicle's very essence.

Maya felt the weight of unseen eyes upon her, scrutiny that sought to peel back her layers of resolve and expose the trembling core beneath. The air around them grew charged, an electric anticipation for the rebellion they plotted against their relentless captor. The interior lights flickered, casting macabre shadows that writhed and twisted, mimicking nightmares best left untouched.

"Stay true to your course, no matter the mind's protests," Ben said, his gaze unwavering even as the bus contorted around them, its geometry an affront to nature's laws.

She could feel it — the sinister will of the bus clawing at her determination, tendrils of doubt attempting to pry into her thoughts. It was as though the beast itself sensed their imminent exodus, rousing from slumber to exert its malignant influence directly upon their psyches.

"Trust in what you know to be real," Ben's voice cut through the burgeoning terror, a beacon of sanity in the chaos that threatened to engulf them. "Trust in me."

As the crossroads drew closer, a maelstrom of supernatural energy swirling at its heart, Maya clutched onto Ben's words like a talisman against the onslaught of despair that the bus conjured with every passing second. Her mind teetered on the precipice, staring down into the abyss that beckoned with a siren's call. But it was Ben's presence — solid, unyielding — that anchored her to reality.

The beast roared beneath them, a final attempt to snare its prey. But Maya and Ben stood resolute, two souls intertwined by fate and the shared desire for freedom. And when the moment came, they would leap together, defying the malevolent force that sought to claim them for eternity.

Whispers ceased between Maya and Ben, a heavy silence falling over them as the bus lurched forward, its wheels turning with wicked intent. A thickening air congealed around Maya, each breath she drew laden with a nameless dread. It was as if the very atmosphere conspired to suffocate their plans before they could unfurl wings of escape.

She felt it then, a creeping numbness in her fingertips, a sign of the oxygen-thin environment wrapping itself around her slender frame. Maya's chest tightened, her lungs laboring against the oppressive shroud that threatened to smother the life from her. She dared not let her gaze wander to the other passengers, those inhuman entities that watched with eyes gleaming like shards of onyx set in the visage of nightmares.

Ben's hand found hers, a touch that should have been comforting but felt as cold as the space between stars. "Keep breathing," he urged, though his breaths came shallow and ragged. "Remember who you are."

This was another puzzle, albeit one cloaked in shadows and woven of threads pulled from the fabric of insanity. The rhythm of her heart became the metronome by which she measured the waning moments. Maya, the diligent scholar, could not—would not—yield to the phantasms of fear. She refocused, her eyes a lighthouse piercing through the fog of terror. The darkness need not be her end but rather the crucible in which her essence was refined.

In the face of the unrelenting darkness, she held fast to Ben's advice and used it to steel her spine against the malignancy that seeped from every sinew of the bus. They would make their stand, not as victims to be devoured by despair, but as architects of their salvation. For in the end, was it not the nature of the beast to underestimate its prey? And was it not the nature of humanity to rise, even when breath and hope grew scarce?

As the bus snaked its way toward an unseen terminus, Maya clung to her determination. It was a fragile thing, beset on all sides by the weight of her doubts and the suffocating air. Yet it was also unyielding, a testament to the strength that lay at the core of her being—a strength that would see her through the darkest of rides.

Maya's thoughts splintered as visions of cosmic dread tore through the fabric of her reality. Ghostly tentacles of darkness writhed in the corners of her eyes, a grotesque ballet of inhuman forms that defied both physics and sanity. The bus seemed to stretch into infinity, its narrow aisle an impossible chasm between the realms of living and dead. She felt the breath of something ancient and evil upon her neck, whispering promises of eternal oblivion in a chorus of voices stolen from forgotten nightmares.

The air twisted around her, thickening with each passing moment, as if the atmosphere itself sought to smother the life from her lungs. She heard the faintest echo of Ben's voice, but it was lost within the cacophony of unearthly howls that clawed at the edges of her mind. A chilling realization crept over Maya, one that danced mockingly upon the precipice of her understanding: they were not alone on this journey—the very essence of the universe was aware of their presence, and it hungered.

Waves of despair crashed against the shores of her will, each surge laced with images of monstrosities so vile that they threatened to unravel the very essence of her being. Yet amidst this onslaught, Maya's intellect proved a defiant beacon, casting its analytical glow upon the shadows that sought to consume her. Her studies had always been a fortress of reason; now they became her armor against the madness, each memory a bulwark against the terror that besieged her.

As the bus approached the crossroads, the world outside transformed. It was no mere intersection of roads but rather a confluence of realities, a maelstrom of energies that swirled with the colors of chaos. Here, the veil was thin, and the fabric of existence trembled with the touch of things unseen. The landscape churned and morphed, an ever-shifting tapestry of eldritch design, where the sky bled into the earth, and stars blinked with malefic intent.

The crossroads stretched out before them, a veritable abyss lined by the gnarled trees of some petrified forest, their branches clawing at the void above. The air was alive with the hum of power, a symphony of whispers that resonated with the pulse of other dimensions. It was a place untethered from time, where past sins and future damnations converged in a silent scream of eternal resonance.

Maya's resolve wavered for the briefest of moments, her scholarly composure fraying at the edges as she stared into the heart of the nexus. But then, steeling herself against the fear that clawed at her soul, she summoned forth the remnants of her courage. Whatever lay beyond the crossroads, whatever trials awaited in the folds of the infinite, she would face them head-on. For knowledge, once ignited within the human spirit, is a flame that not even the darkest abyss can extinguish.

CHAPTER 8
APPROACHING THE CROSSROADS

THE HOLLOW ROUTE

The air itself seemed to tremble with anticipation, a silent overture to the madness that awaited them. Outside, reality fractured, the serene countryside splintering into fragments of existence that bled into one another like watercolors caught in the rain. A landscape once familiar now bore the scars of unearthly intrusion—a forest with trees twisted into grotesque shapes, a sky painted with the swirling colors of a stormy sea, and buildings that flickered between decrepit ruins and modern façades in the blink of an eye. Maya's breath caught in her throat as she witnessed time and space contort, intertwining like lovers locked in a macabre dance orchestrated by unseen forces.

"Stay focused, Maya," Ben whispered beside her, his voice a tether in the tempest that sought to claim her senses. His gaunt face, usually a mask of haunted resilience, was now etched with concern for the young scholar who had become his unexpected charge in this nightmare realm.

The driver sat at the helm, his skeletal hands steady despite the anarchy that unfolded outside the windows. The pallor of his skin seemed to blend with the ethereal light that seeped through the cracks in reality, rendering him more specter than man.

Maya's heart thrummed, a staccato beat against the

eerie silence that surrounded them. She dared not look too long into the abyss beyond the fractured glass lest she lose herself entirely to the hypnotic discord of worlds colliding. Her mind recoiled at the sight, yet her academic curiosity itched to unravel the mysteries of this liminal space — a place where the veil was torn asunder, revealing the raw edges of the universe.

"Keep your eyes here, with me," Ben's voice broke through again, grounding her spiraling thoughts. In the periphery, shadows danced and coalesced, hinting at forms both terrifying and familiar, but she heeded his warning, focusing on the rhythm of her breathing and the solidity of the seat beneath her.

As the bus careened toward its enigmatic destination, the crossroads of reality and nightmare, Maya clung to the remnants of her sanity. For beyond the shattered windowpane lay truths too harrowing for the human soul, and Maya, armed with intellect and determination, was not yet ready to succumb to their siren call.

The engine's growl deepened, thrumming through the vehicle like a predator's purr, as the bus twisted upon an unseen axis, contorting with the elegance of a creature stretching its limbs after a long slumber. At once, Maya felt the shift, her senses piqued by the grotesque ballet of steel and shadows. She was acutely aware that the mundane guise of public transport had sloughed away, revealing the grotesquerie beneath.

"Focus, Maya," she whispered to herself, the words a lifeline thrown into the churning sea of her thoughts. Her voice sounded foreign, swallowed up by the chorus of whispers that began to weave around her, an insidious tapestry of sound. The murmurs were not loud, but they bore the weight of graves, each syllable a stone upon her chest.

"Unworthy," hissed one spectral voice, close enough to raise the hairs on her nape.

"Lost," another taunted, as if it floated down from the very heavens to mock her.

Maya pressed her palms into the cool leather of the seat, grounding herself in its tangible reality. Yet, her eyes, lamps in the gathering gloom, betrayed her unrest. They flickered, not with fear, but with determination as they dissected each whisper for its source, its intent.

"Resist them," Ben urged, a rock amidst the storm. His steady gaze implored her to anchor herself to something more substantial than the phantasmagoria that sought to claim her.

The bus — no longer a mere bus — writhed as it trundled onward. Its frame shrieked like an orchestra of metallic agony as rivets popped and panels bulged. To look upon, it was to witness a metamorphosis too hideous for daylight's comfort yet too mesmerizing to avert one's gaze. It was becoming something else, something that the well of human nightmares had eagerly relinquished.

"Look away," Ben muttered, though whether it was for her benefit or his own, the darkness kept secret.

Maya did not look away. She could not. Her eyes, those twin pools of verdant depth, saw past the horror to the pattern beneath. A scholar's curiosity is a double-edged sword, sharp enough to cleave through ignorance yet often drawn toward the perilous allure of forbidden knowledge.

"Maya," the voices cooed, a symphony of despair, "embrace the void."

"Never," she breathed, her lips barely parting. Her heart was a drumbeat in a dirge, yet it hammered out a rhythm of defiance. In this macabre convergence of worlds, amid the cacophony of the damned and the creaking bones of the bus, Maya held fast to the essence of who she was — a beacon of reason in a universe that laughed at such things.

And so, as the crossroads loomed, a vortex where dreams and nightmares waltzed together, Maya steeled herself against the coming maelstrom, her mind a fortress besieged by ghosts of doubt and dread.

The bus's journey into the abyss marched on the road to perdition. The passengers, once mere shadows within its confines, began a grotesque transformation under the baleful gaze of an unseen moon. Shapes twisted, limbs elongated with the crackle of breaking bones, faces contorted into silent screams etched by an invisible chisel of terror.

Maya watched, her breath caught in her throat as a man, not two seats ahead, unraveled like a spool of thread, his very essence unwinding into a mass of spectral tendrils that writhed in unholy animation. A woman to her side faded into a translucent wraith, her mouth agape in a silent howl that threatened to swallow the remaining sliver of sanity Maya clung to.

"Close your eyes," Ben whispered, his voice barely piercing the cacophony of silent shrieks and whispers. Yet she could not — would not — turn away from this phantasmal horror show.

The driver stood at the heart of this chaos, unchanging amidst the storm of transformations. His form, however, was betraying an alliance with the malevolent entity they rode within. With each mile devoured by the ghastly vehicle, he seemed to sink deeper into its structure, his pallid skin merging with the sinewy metal, veins melding with cables in a perverse symbiosis.

His hands, once clearly defined against the steering wheel, now appeared fused to it, his fingers lengthening and curling around the spokes like ivy claiming an ancient wall. The uniform that had clung to him like a ghost of his past life now rippled and flowed into the bus's fabric, a tapestry of souls lost and bound together in eternal servitude.

"Part of the machine," Ben muttered, his eyes never leaving the driver, who was no longer a man but an extension of the infernal contraption itself.

The air grew thick with the scent of fire and brimstone, a noxious perfume that heralded the proximity of the crossroads. It was a place where the weary and the damned found their paths entwined, a junction of fates forever forked between oblivion and eternity. As the driver and the bus became one, the windows revealed vistas of other worlds bleeding into one another—a kaleidoscope of nightmares where sky and earth were indiscernible. The once-solid reality buckled under the weight of the spectral onslaught, and within the eye of this maelstrom, Maya felt the tug of something far more terrifying than the ghosts that surrounded her: the seduction of surrender to the void. But still, she held firm, her resolve a lighthouse beam cutting through the fog of fear.

And there, in the center of it all, the crossroads waited, a maw ready to devour or deliver, depending on the offering laid at its threshold. The world outside the bus fractured, a mirror shattering into a thousand reflections of reality. Maya's heartbeat thrummed in her ears, each pulse an echo of Ben's teachings — the mantra that had become her armor against the encroaching madness. "Remember who you are," he'd said, his voice a beacon in the tempest of her mind. "Hold fast to your truth."

Clutching these words to her chest like a talisman, Maya wrestled with the visions that now assailed her. Memories of home flickered before her eyes: the familiar warmth of sunlight streaming through her bedroom window, the comforting scent of old books lining her shelves, the laughter of loved ones echoing in the halls—each a seductive whisper promising safety.

"Focus, Maya," she chided herself, the sound of her own voice a lifeline amidst the whispers seeking to ensnare her. The faces of spectral entities leered from the periphery, their ghastly forms undulating with malevolent intent. Yet, it was not their grotesque appearances that threatened her most but the insidious allure of complacency they sought to instill.

A spectral hand reached out, its touch cold as the abyss, and Maya recoiled. She could feel the pull, the temptation to let go, to succumb to the ease of oblivion where no terror could touch her. For a fleeting moment, her resolve wavered like a candle flame in the wind.

But then she remembered—Ben's haunted eyes, the weight of his experiences etched into every line on his face, his relentless fight despite the odds. He was a testament to the human spirit's enduring strength, a reminder that surrender was not her only option.

"Fight, Maya," Ben's voice echoed in her memory, a ghostly incantation against the darkness. "You are more than this place, more than its lies."

And so, she fought. Each vision of home dissolved into the miasma, a dream dispelled by the dawn's merciless light. Maya anchored herself to the present, to the grim certainty of the spectral bus and the uneven rhythm of its journey towards a destination unknown.

"Home is behind me," she whispered, her voice steady despite the chaos. "I am here. I am Maya Scott, and I will not be unmade."

As the landscape churned and contorted outside, Maya clung to Ben's teachings, her spirit a defiant spark amidst the desolation. She would not yield; she would endure. For in this realm of shadows and sorrow, where even time seemed a prisoner to the whims of darker forces, it was her will alone that carved a path through the encroaching night.

The spectral bus, a prisoner to its own unraveling existence, convulsed as the boundaries of reality frayed at the edges. The world outside, once a blur of passing shadows and half-remembered landscapes, now writhed in a grotesque tapestry of worlds unmeant to meet. Maya's breath caught in her throat; every gasp was a lifeline slipping through her fingers.

"Focus on my voice," Ben urged, his words slicing through the cacophony of whispering voices that curled around Maya's mind like insidious tendrils. His hand found hers — a solid presence in the maelstrom — an anchor against the tide threatening to sweep her away into madness.

Her slender build shivered, vulnerable in the face of such relentless assault, yet tempered by an indomitable will. Maya's piercing eyes, wide with terror, met Ben's haunted gaze. They shared a silent understanding, a communion of spirits tethered amidst the chaos. It was in this moment, entwined with desperation and resolve, that the crossroads unveiled itself.

A swirling vortex of reality and nightmare emerged before them, where all things converged, and none could escape unchanged. The very air trembled, pulsating with the heartbeat of countless dimensions, colliding in a symphony of discordance. Maya felt a pull, a seductive whisper promising solace within the eye of the storm. Her analytical mind grappled with the impossibility, yet her soul knew no logic here could stand. She drew from the well of her education, her love for the tangible truths of her studies now her shield against the intangible horrors before her.

"Remember who you are," Ben's voice resonated, low and steady, a counterpoint to the chaos. Each syllable was a fortress, each pause a sanctuary in the darkness.

"Ben," she murmured, his name a mantra to ward off the phantoms clawing at the edges of her sanity. Her thoughts were a ship adrift, but in his unwavering grasp, she found her harbor. In the labyrinth of her mind, it was Ben's teachings that illuminated the path, a beacon back to herself.

The bus — no longer a mere vehicle but a beast of eldritch design — shuddered and moaned as its true form bled through the guise of mundane metal and glass. The passengers, their humanity stripped away, revealed themselves as spectral entities, each a grotesque mockery of life.

"Look not into the abyss," Ben warned, his voice barely above a whisper yet carrying the weight of his tormented past. His hand tightened around Maya's, a lifeline cast in the darkest sea.

They stood at the precipice, the crossroads beckoning with its enigmatic promise. Maya, with her intellect and resilience, and Ben, with his protective fervor and hard-won wisdom, faced the tempest together. Their bond, forged in adversity, became the crucible in which their fate would be decided.

As the vortex loomed ahead, an unfathomable gateway between worlds, Maya felt the pull of infinite possibilities — and the paralyzing fear of what lay beyond. Would they emerge triumphant, or would they succumb to the creeping horror that sought to claim their very souls? The answer lay waiting in the heart of the storm, where reality and nightmare danced in their eternal, sinister embrace.

CHAPTER 9
THE ESCAPE ATTEMPT

THE HOLLOW ROUTE

The bus's tires shrieked a lament on the forsaken asphalt as it juddered to an abrupt stop at the crossroads, where the fabric of reality seemed to fray and dangle like loose threads of sanity. Around them, the world peeled away in layers, each tear revealing glimpses of places that should not be.

Maya felt the weight of decision press upon her chest, the air thick as if it carried the dust of eons. She shared a glance with Ben, his haunted eyes signaling an unspoken pact. This was their gambit against the lurking shadows that feasted on hope and devoured light. With an exchange of nods, they rose from their seats, determined forms cutting through the murkiness.

"Ready?" Maya's voice, a whisper that somehow defied the oppressive silence, was met by Ben's curt nod.

"Always," he replied, his tone a graveyard of dreams yet a bastion for the courage they would need.

As they moved, an invisible force bore down upon them as though the very air sought to compress their wills into submission. It was a silent adversary, unseen yet palpable, pushing back with the malice of a thousand lost souls. Maya leaned into it, her slender frame belying the strength that pulsed in her veins—a strength born of relentless pursuit of knowledge, of nights spent unraveling enigmas in the cloistered halls of academia.

Ben matched her stride, his movements deliberate, each step a defiance of the spectral chains that had bound him for months beyond counting. His rugged form flickered with the strain as though he were a candle flame caught in a tempestuous wind, struggling to remain alight amidst the encroaching darkness.

Together, they fought against the unseen mire, moving as if through water that grew denser with every inch gained. Reality itself convulsed around them, echoing with the silent screams of those who had traversed this liminal space before and failed.

"Keep going," Ben rasped, his voice barely carrying over the din of the collapsing worlds. "We're close."

The bus, now a mere specter of its former self, creaked ominously, as if mourning its impending loss. Yet the pair trudged onward, their resolve unwavering, even as the specter of oblivion gnawed at their heels.

"Can't...let it...win," Maya gasped, her breath coming in short, sharp intakes as she battled the unseen resistance, every fiber of her being urging her towards escape—and freedom.

The tendrils curled forth like fingers of the damned, their wispy forms grasping at Maya's ankles with a chilling tenacity. The spectral filaments, spawned from the abyss that had claimed the bus at the crossroads, were insatiable in their quest to drag the living back into their fold. Each touch was an icy whisper against Maya's skin, a plea from the void that hungered for her vitality.

"Ben!" she cried out, her voice laced with an edge of panic as she felt the numbing grip of ethereal energy seeking to ensnare her very soul. She was an academic, a mind accustomed to the clarity of reason and the tangibility of facts, yet here she stood, besieged by forces that defied all logic.

"Keep moving," Ben grunted, his form shimmering as if he were a mirage on the brink of being dispelled by reality. His presence was a beacon of hope in the maelstrom, a testament to human resilience against the impossible. Yet the toll of this place gnawed at him, casting shadows across his gaunt face as if each moment stretched him thinner between worlds.

Maya's heart pounded, her resolve a fortress amidst the encroaching despair. With each step towards the exit, the air grew heavier, a thick veil of resistance that clung to them like the remnants of a nightmare. Her muscles screamed in protest, her thoughts a tempest of fear and determination.

"Fight it, Maya," Ben urged, his voice a lifeline thrown across the chasm of uncertainty. He moved with dogged perseverance, the very image of a man who had become intimate with specters and phantoms, his survival a dance with death itself.

Their advance was a torturous slog, the bus's interior now a theater of horrors where the ordinary became sinister, and the exit loomed as a distant beacon of salvation. Every breath Maya drew seemed laced with the cold dread that filled the space, each exhalation a release of the terror that sought to claim her.

"Almost there," she whispered, more to herself than to Ben, her words an incantation to ward off the dread that slithered along the edges of her consciousness. The tendrils recoiled with each utterance, as though her voice carried a power they feared, a reminder that she was still anchored to the world of the living.

And so they persisted, two souls bound by shared desperation, inching closer to the threshold beyond which lay the promise of escape — or the peril of deeper entrapment. The gothic tableau of their plight, set against the backdrop of the spectral bus, was a grim reminder that some borders, once crossed, demand a toll that can never be repaid in full.

"Keep moving!" Ben barked, his voice a life raft to which Maya clung amidst the swirling torrent of other realms. The bus, no longer merely a vehicle but a vessel adrift in a sea of nightmarish possibility, jerked and swayed as if protesting their advance.

From the shifting shadows, hands emerged—translucent appendages wrought from the very fog that filled the bus. They clutched at Maya's clothes and her hair, desperate to drag her into their ranks. Spectral passengers, prisoners of the route unending, faces devoid of hope or recognition, reached for her with a longing born of eternal wandering.

"Let go!" she cried, tearing herself free from one cold grasp only to find another latching onto her. Her heart hammered a dirge against her ribs, the rhythm of a soul knowing it might soon join this ghostly tableau.

Ben's hand found hers, grip ironclad, a lifeline amidst the phantoms. He pulled her forward, though his own form seemed to waver with the effort, caught between two worlds, a half-remembered name on a gravestone overgrown with ivy.

"Stay with me," he urged, though who he implored—the haunted or the haunter—remained unsaid.

The air itself howled a mournful cry that claimed kinship with every forgotten ghost. Maya fixed her gaze on the narrowing sliver of reality that remained constant—the exit, a mere whisper of light, a promise so fragile it could shatter with a breath.

"Almost..." she gasped, the word a fragile thing, threatened to be lost in the cacophony of liminal space. They were close now, so perilously close, the boundary of their prison within reach. Would it be a release, or would the crossing demand a price too steep?

Beside her, Ben was struggling under his invisible burden. His form flickered uncertainly, like the flame of a candle buffeted by unseen winds. Months of entrapment within this spectral vessel had woven him into its fabric, the lines that tethered him to their reality fraying with each passing moment. Maya could see it in the way his image wavered, a ghostly double exposure on the film of the world. "Ben!"

"Keep moving," he ground out, the command roughened by his desperation. His eyes, those haunted wells of experience, locked onto hers — unyielding, commanding her to endure.

She stumbled, nearly falling prey once again to the predatory energy that suffused the air. It clawed at her resolve, lapping at the edges of her consciousness like a black tide, whispering seductions of surrender. But Maya's spirit, tempered in the crucible of knowledge and honed by the sharp edge of curiosity, would not yield so easily.

"Focus on me, Maya." His voice was a lifeline thrown across the chasm of madness. He reached for her again with hands that seemed to phase in and out of solidity, grasping for the tangible when all around them was ephemeral.

"Can't..." Her breath came in ragged gasps, and she felt the inexorable pull toward the void, a siren call to join the chorus of lost souls that surrounded them. She resisted, thinking of her family, her ambitions, and the life that awaited beyond this cursed conveyance.

Ben's struggle was more profound, the specter of the bus having sunk its claws deep into his psyche, claiming him as its own. With each effort to pull away, the entity that held him captive tightened its grip, a jealously possessive lover refusing to relinquish its claim. Yet still, he persisted, driven by a protective fervor that defied the darkness that sought to consume him.

They were two souls entwined in a dance of defiance, moving through a landscape that belonged to neither the living nor the dead. The air hung heavy with the sorrow of eons, the walls of the bus vibrating with the silent screams of the trapped. Still, they pressed onward toward the sliver of hope that beckoned them from the threshold of their nightmare.

"Almost there," Maya whispered, though whether it was encouragement or a desperate incantation, even she could not tell. In the murk of shifting realities, where time itself seemed to bleed into nothingness, every step was a victory hard-won against the forces that sought to bind them to this place of shadows.

The spectral wail rent the fabric of silence, a sound so hideous it seemed to claw at the very air. Maya's heart thundered in her chest, its rhythm erratic as if mirroring the chaos that encroached upon them. With the howl came a coldness, a chill that promised the touch of death should they falter. The cry echoed, bouncing off unseen walls, magnifying until it was all she could hear—a cacophony of despair from the abyss clawing at their heels.

"Keep moving!" Ben's voice cut through the din, his form flickering like a flame under a tempest's fury. His eyes held fast to hers, two beacons in the gloom that beseeched her not to give in to the terror that sought to paralyze them.

The other passengers, now less than shadows—less than memories—reached out with grasping, spectral hands, yearning for the life force that Maya and Ben fought so valiantly to preserve. There was a cruel irony in their desperation, the dead seeking solace in the warmth of the living, even as they unwittingly conspired to snuff it out.

As they neared the threshold of salvation, Ben staggered, his essence wavering dangerously close to dissolution, a testament to the price paid for lingering too long in limbo. "Go!" he gasped, the word more plea than command, his haunted gaze imploring Maya to seize the chance that he might not grasp.

Maya, driven by a survival instinct honed in the crucible of her scholarly challenges, mustered a resolve that defied the supernatural forces arrayed against them. Her mind, sharpened by years of analytical thought, refused to succumb to the madness that beckoned. She knew that to hesitate would be to join the legion of lost souls, to become one more whisper in the chorus of anguish.

With a final, desperate lunge, she reached for the exit, her hand outstretched, fingers brushing against the promise of escape. The door loomed before them, a portal back to the world of the living—a boundary that marked the end of their ordeal or the beginning of eternal damnation. It stood, indifferent to their plight, a silent arbiter of fate.

"NOW!" she cried, a clarion call that pierced the suffocating dread. Together, Maya and Ben threw themselves forward, bodies and spirits colliding with the door that stood as the only barrier to their freedom.

For a moment that stretched into infinity, there was only darkness, a void where hope and despair danced in a macabre embrace. Then, with a shudder that reverberated through the core of their beings, the door yielded, and they spilled forth from the mouth of the beast, tumbling into the world they had almost forgotten.

Freedom embraced them, sweet and sharp as the first breath after a plunge into icy depths.

CHAPTER 10
BEYOND THE VEIL

THE HOLLOW ROUTE

Maya's reality splintered as she and Ben, her unwitting compatriot in this descent into the unfathomable, tumbled out of the spectral bus. They landed hard upon the ground at the crossroads—a nexus of half-remembered dreams and whispered fears, where the fabric of existence was worn thin.

The earth beneath them refused to hold still. It revolved with a sickening lurch, an old carousel of distorted landscapes spinning faster and faster into a blur. Maya's breath hitched as she struggled to find solid ground amidst the churning madness. This was not the hallowed halls of academia nor the comforting embrace of a family; it was a place that defied all logic and reason, a place unbound by the constraints of her sharp intellect.

Ben's voice, a beacon of human warmth in the cold whirlwind of chaos, cut through the disorienting spectacle. "Focus on my voice, Maya," he urged, his words tinged with the wisdom of one who had navigated these treacherous waters before. His eyes, those portals to a soul marred by otherworldly horrors, searched hers for acknowledgment.

Around them, the world convulsed with the agony of a thousand colliding realities. Shadows danced like frenzied specters, merging and splitting with reckless abandon. The sound was deafening—the roar of unseen oceans, the wail of lost spirits, the crackle of time itself fraying at the edges.

Maya dug deep within herself past the fear and the overwhelming sense of smallness in the face of such incomprehensible forces. She summoned the persistence that had always been her compass, the resourcefulness that had seen her through countless late nights buried in books and theories.

"Where are we?" she managed to ask, her voice a mere whisper swallowed by the cacophony around them. But perhaps there were no words to describe this place, no earthly language that could encapsulate its raw, primordial essence.

"Between," Ben replied, his voice strained but resolute. "Between what is known and what should never be glimpsed."

And as they stood at the precipice of sanity, the very ground beneath their feet seemed to pulse with a life of its own, throbbing with the heartbeat of a universe in turmoil. The crossroads stretched out in every direction yet offered no clear path, only the certainty that whatever choice they made would change them irrevocably.

In the guttural choir of the abyss, the pair found themselves adrift, each seeking an anchor in the tempestuous sea of unreality. What lay ahead was unknown, and what lay behind was a doorway forever closed, sealed with the echoes of their haunted pasts.

Maya's fingers laced through Ben's with an urgency that betrayed her scholarly calm. Around them, the world twisted in a grotesque mockery of reality, shadows and light bleeding into each other with unnatural fluidity. They clung to one another, two souls attempting to tether their existence to something tangible amidst the chaos that threatened to dissolve the very fabric of their beings.

"Stay with me," Maya implored, her voice a fragile thread weaving through the oppressive silence that followed the storm. The sound seemed almost too delicate for this place as if the mere act of speaking could fracture the brittle air around them.

Ben's grip tightened, his protective nature a bulwark against the maddening energies that sought to unmake them. "Not going anywhere," he promised, though the words hung heavily between them, a harbinger of promises made in realms where such vows could be torn asunder like cobwebs.

The bus, that infernal vessel of spectral wanderings, convulsed behind them. It was a beast in its death throes, or perhaps it was merely angry, its steel body warping in ways that defied the laws of physics. Windows melted into eyes that blinked with malevolent intent, and the doors gnashed like the maw of some ravenous creature, eager to swallow its quarry whole once more.

It was a sight to unravel the mind, and Maya felt the first tendrils of panic creep like ivy around her thoughts. She had always found comfort in the rational, explainable phenomena of the universe. But here, logic held no dominion; here, only madness reigned.

"Look away," Ben muttered, his gaze fixed on some distant point of salvation that Maya couldn't yet see. He understood the dangers of this place better than most, the way it whispered sweet lunacies into the ears of the unwary until there was nothing left but the echo of their distorted laughter.

With each contortion, the bus let out a cacophony of metallic groans and shrieks, a symphony of despair that resonated with the anguish of every lost soul it had ever claimed. Its form blurred at the edges, flickering in and out of existence as if even it wasn't certain of its shape any longer. The crossroads around them seemed to respond to its agony, a macabre dance of reality bending to the will of something far older and far crueler than anything Maya had ever dared to contemplate in her studies.

"Keep your eyes on me," she told Ben, her scholarly resolve hardened into a shield against the encroaching dread. Her eyes, usually so full of curiosity, now bore the weight of a thousand unseen horrors, reflecting a determination forged in the heart of a nightmare.

They stood, two figures defiant in the face of oblivion, holding on to each other as if their shared warmth could ward off the cold touch of the crossroads. And all the while, the bus writhed behind them, its form becoming less and less coherent, a dark smudge against a backdrop of swirling ether, desperate to drag them back into its fold of eternal wandering.

The world swirled in a tempest of shadows and light, reality itself splintering at the seams. Maya and Ben stumbled through the tumult, their hands clasped with a desperation born of terror. The crossroads churned around them, an abyss where countless realities clashed and fought for dominance. The ground beneath their feet was no more reliable than the whispers of insanity that threatened to overtake their minds.

"Ben," Maya gasped, her voice barely audible above the roar of colliding dimensions. "We—we have to focus. Find something real, anchor ourselves."

Her words were a lifeline thrown into the void. Ben nodded, his haunted eyes scanning the chaos. They sought solace in each other's grip as if their linked fingers could weave a spell strong enough to withstand the assault on their senses. Ben's presence, rugged and worn, stood as a testament to human resilience amidst the supernatural onslaught.

"Look!" he cried, pointing towards a sliver of calm in the eye of the metaphysical storm. A faint outline shimmered there, a tear in the fabric of the maelstrom—a path that seemed to lead away from this place of madness.

Maya followed his gaze, her intellect cutting through

the fog of fear. She discerned patterns in the pandemonium, the methodical academic within mapping constellations in the swirling energies. There was a rhythm to the chaos, a cadence that sang of escape—if one knew how to listen.

"Towards the light," she urged, her voice a steady drumbeat against the wails of the crossroads. "That's our way out."

Together, they moved, their steps tentative yet purpose-driven. The path home coalesced with each labored breath, the promise of reality growing stronger, a beacon cutting through the oppressive gloom. It was a narrow passage, bordered by the remnants of fractured worlds, but it was a chance—an opportunity to flee the relentless clutches of the spectral bus and its eternal route of despair.

The ground solidified beneath them as they drew closer, the path emerging like a forgotten trail rediscovered. At their approach, the energies whirled faster, as though the crossroads resented their defiance, yet the path held firm—a silent challenge to the forces that sought to keep them trapped.

"Almost there," Ben murmured, his voice a raw whisper of hope. "Just hold on, Maya."

But the path was jealous of its secrets, reluctant to yield its end to mere mortals. With every step they took, the darkness clawed at their heels, a reminder of the sins and sorrows that had led them to this precipice between worlds. And even as salvation beckoned, the shadow of the crossroads loomed large behind them, ready to swallow them whole should they falter.

"Keep moving," Maya insisted, her resolve unyielding. They were close now, so close to piercing the veil and reclaiming the lives they had been torn from. Yet even as they neared the threshold, the echoes of their past misdeeds whispered through the wind, a haunting refrain meant to unnerve and ensnare.

Their footsteps quickened, hearts pounding in sync with the frenzied tempo of their escape. They dared not look back, for the past was a specter best left behind, and the future — a glimmer of light amidst the dark — was all that mattered now.

The spectral bus, once a vehicle of twisted iron and despair, began to writhe as though it were a creature of flesh and bone. Its shriek was the sound of metal on metal, a symphony of agony that clawed at Maya's ears with icy fingers. With each grotesque contortion, the bus shrank into itself, folding like some dark origami trick gone horribly awry.

"Run!" Ben's voice tore through the cacophony, a beacon of urgency that set their limbs to motion. His hand gripped hers with a strength that defied his gaunt appearance, the sinews in his arm taut as they sprinted toward the flickering promise of reality. The path before them was narrow, fraught with the whispers of shadows that sought to disorient and ensnare.

Maya could feel the ground beneath her begin to give way, as if the very earth were reluctant to bear the weight of their escape. She stumbled, her pulse a frantic drumbeat in her throat, but Ben's grip was unyielding. They pushed onward, the path now a blur beneath their desperate strides.

"Almost there." The words were a mantra upon Ben's lips, spoken as much to convince himself as to encourage Maya. Each syllable was infused with the terror and hope that had become their shared currency in this forsaken place.

The air thickened around them, heavy with the stench of oblivion, pressing down upon their chests until each breath became a battle. Yet they did not relent, driven by the raw instinct to survive, to witness the sunrise once more upon a world untainted by the madness that pursued them.

As they neared the threshold where realities converged, the fabric of the crossroads trembled. It threatened to unravel completely, the seams of existence coming undone under the strain of their defiance. But Maya and Ben, united by the scars of their journey, lent no credence to the fear that gnawed at their resolve.

With one final surge of determination, they lunged forward, crossing the intangible boundary that separated nightmare from waking life. The last echoes of the bus's death wail faded into an oppressive silence as they breached the veil, leaving behind the twisted crossroads where time and space had lost all meaning.

The ground beneath Maya and Ben's feet buckled and split, a chasm of non-existence yawning wide to swallow the last vestiges of the crossroads. Screams from the void clawed at their backs, spectral fingers grasping for purchase on their reality.

"Run!" Maya's voice was a harsh whisper, her breaths ragged as she felt the fabric of the world tearing away behind them. She dared not glance back for fear that the sight would unravel her mind as easily as the collapsing planes unraveled around them.

Ben's hand gripped hers with an intensity that left no room for doubt or hesitation. His gaunt frame belied the strength that surged through him as he propelled them both toward the shimmering outline of their world—a beacon in the engulfing darkness that threatened to consume all.

The air around them shuddered, a palpable sense of displacement washing over the pair in waves. The crossroads gave one final, violent shudder, a soundless implosion that promised oblivion to any soul caught within its maw. It was a narrow escape, a hair's breadth between salvation and eternal damnation.

And then, suddenly, the chaos receded. The cold grip of the otherworldly loosened, replaced by the mundane chill of a nighttime breeze. They stumbled onto solid pavement, the familiar sights of the city bleeding into view like ink into parchment.

Maya's eyes, once filled with the vibrant thirst for knowledge, now held the haunted reflection of too many secrets laid bare. She stood beside Ben, their silhouettes etched against the backdrop of a world that seemed too simple, too benign to have ever contained the horrors they had just escaped.

"Is it...over?" Ben's voice cracked, carrying the weight of months spent in a limbo that had tested the limits of his resolve, reshaping him into a sentinel marked by trials unknown to his former self.

"Perhaps." Maya's reply was a mere whisper, her intellect grappling with the impossibility of what they had endured. "But we are altered, aren't we? The things we saw..."

"Can't be unseen," Ben finished for her, his weary eyes scanning the empty street, half expecting the twisted form of the bus to materialize once more.

Their shared ordeal had carved a bond between them, deeper than understanding, beyond the realm of spoken words. They knew, without needing to articulate it, that the echoes of those shrieking wheels, the ghostly wails of trapped souls, would forever linger in the silence of their darkest nights.

As they walked away from the spot where two realities had once collided, they did so with the heavy gait of survivors—of specters who had glimpsed the abyss and carried its shadow within them. Their journey back to the normalcy of their lives would be fraught with whispers of doubt, fleeting shadows at the edge of vision, and the unshakable feeling of being watched by unseen eyes.

The world around them continued its oblivious spin, but for Maya and Ben, every step taken was a testament to their harrowing passage through the veil—and their return was not a homecoming but the beginning of a haunting that would endure long after the crossroads had collapsed into nothingness.

Erik Daniel Shein, originally born as Erik Daniel Stoops in Northfield, Ohio, emerges as a visionary storyteller deeply captivated by the paranormal and a fervent champion for animal welfare. His artistic flair spans various genres, seamlessly merging his love for storytelling with a profound commitment to animation and the welfare of animals.

Erik's odyssey in the realms of publishing and animal welfare commenced alongside editor Sheila Ann Barry at Sterling Publications. Together, they crafted six non-fiction children's books about animals, presented in an engaging question-and-answer format. His exploration extended to the fascinating field of herpetology, where he refined his expertise as a trained authority on reptiles and amphibians.

As a consultant for both local and federal fish and wildlife services, Erik immersed himself in the intricate world of these creatures, contributing invaluable insights to conservation endeavors. This rich background served as the bedrock for his eventual transition into the enthralling realms of written and visual storytelling.

Melissa Davis is an accomplished multi-genre author with over 50 novels and numerous screenplays to her credit. Born in Southern Illinois, her lifelong passion for reading inspired her to begin writing creatively at the age of seven. She further developed her talent while attending the prestigious Illinois Summer School for the Arts during high school. Melissa went on to graduate with a Bachelor's in Education from Illinois State University. She initially worked as a teacher before leaving to focus on raising her children and pursuing her dream of becoming a full-time writer.

As a multi-genre author, Melissa's novels span a diverse range, including contemporary and historical fiction, fantasy, mystery, and more. With over twenty years of experience, she is an expert in crafting intricate plot lines and multi-dimensional characters that resonate with readers across genres. Her writing has been praised by critics and readers alike for its warmth, insight, and ability to capture the full range of human emotion. When not writing her next book, Melissa enjoys connecting with her loyal community of readers.

Karen Fuller is an award-winning and accomplished multi-genre author with over 30 novels and numerous screenplays to her credit. A graduate of Pensacola State College with an Associate of Arts degree in Business Management, Karen has turned her creative passion into a successful writing career spanning over two decades.

Born in Alabama, Karen began writing at a young age, inspired by her voracious reading habit. After starting a family, she devoted herself to raising her children while continuing to write in her free time. In 2011, Karen took her entrepreneurial spirit further by founding her own publishing press, World Castle Publishing, to provide support and guidance to aspiring authors.

When not crafting intricately woven plotlines brimming with multidimensional characters, Karen enjoys traveling the country to meet her loyal readers at book events. She also loves experiencing the outdoors while camping and watching auto races. Married for over 40 years, Karen now splits her time between writing novels, running her business, and visiting her two grown children and young grandchildren, who provide endless inspiration.

Karen writes in a diverse range of fictional genres, effortlessly transitioning from thriller to romance, dystopian to fantasy. Her novels have received numerous accolades for capturing universal emotions and showcasing the breadth of the human experience. Driven by her imaginative spirit, there is no literary terrain Karen Fuller cannot expertly explore.